The Christmas Invitation

By Kate Kasch

For Liliana

Chapter One

Pinching her nose with one hand, Isabella "Ella" Martinez pushed the door to the men's bathroom, bracing herself for the onslaught of smells. Still holding her breath, she dragged in the bucket of soapy water, the mop, and carrier full of cleaning supplies. This bathroom on the 22nd floor was always the grossest; if only to get it over with, Ella cleaned it first every time she worked.

She removed one rubber glove to turn up the volume on her phone before Christmas music blasted through her earbuds. Then, with the rubber glove back in place, she forged on. Like a machine, she went through the motions of wiping the mirrors and scrubbing the sinks, her mind on a million other things. She had always been good at compartmentalizing. She might be in a stinky men's bathroom at seven o'clock at night wearing a maid's uniform, but her mind was in a happy place.

She thought about the class discussion in her Early Elementary course that morning, and the new Christmas book she was reading on her train ride into Manhattan from Queens. Before she even realized it, the once nasty bathroom was sparkling from floor to ceiling. With one last glance to be sure she hadn't missed anything, Ella walked out of the bathroom and closed the door behind her with a feeling of satisfaction.

Although this job was not what she pictured for herself, she would admit that she enjoyed that feeling of accomplishment at completing the tasks. She was proud of how efficiently and effectively she could clean up any mess. Which was nice because the law offices of Dawson and Hancock were always a mysterious disaster. Ever since her father passed away a couple of years ago, Ella had been working nights cleaning offices. She had seen her fair share of filth, but the 22nd floor of the skyscraper at 430 Fifth Avenue took dirty to a whole other level.

After cleaning the women's bathroom, which was usually in good shape to start with, likely because there were fewer women that worked in the office than men, Ella made her way down the hallway toward the main office area. In the large open space, shoulder-height partitions were jammed together to create a maze of cubicles. Setting the bucket and mop aside, Ella pulled out the vacuum to get started on the beige carpet that was full of crumbs, papers, and pine needles this time of year. As she was about to turn on the vacuum, she felt someone grab her arm. Caught totally by surprise, Ella jumped in the air, pulling her earbuds out of her ears as she moved.

"You really shouldn't listen to that music so loudly," Rosie said, shaking her head in disapproval.

"Geez, Rosie, you scared me to death! Don't sneak up on me like that!"

"I didn't sneak up on you! I called out your name about ten times! It's not my fault that you insist on blasting music straight into your ears. By the time you're my age your hearing is going to be gone." Rosie continued to shake her head. "Mark my words. You keep it up and you won't be able to hear a thing."

"Is there something you needed besides lecturing me on my loud music?" Ella jabbed a fisted hand onto her hip.

"I was going to ask you if you would mind cleaning some of the big offices for me today? I was hoping to cut out a little early. It's Marco's Christmas concert at school tonight and I don't want to miss it."

Marco was Rosie's grandson and the apple of her eye. Ella considered Rosie stubborn, cynical, and a bit of a complainer. But when she talked about Marco, the frown that had taken up permanent residence on Rosie's face disappeared.

"Most people don't lecture someone right before asking for a favor," Ella raised an eyebrow. Rosie's face didn't move. "You know I don't mind. I wouldn't want you missing Marco's performance."

Rosie's face still didn't move. "Thank you. And remember to check all the Christmas trees to see if they need water." With that, she turned around and left to get her coat.

"You're welcome!" Ella called after her. Rosie kept walking without even a glance backward or a nod to acknowledge she heard anything. Ella sighed, put her earbuds back in her ears, and started the vacuum. It looked like it was going to be a long night.

An hour or so later, having finished cleaning the cubicles, Ella started on the individual offices. The offices belonged to the higher-ups, each one getting larger and more lavish with every pay grade. Although they were more work to clean, Ella preferred the larger offices to the cramped cubicles out on the floor.

Each office told a story about its occupant. The photos of ski trips, beach vacations, smiling families, and beautiful women were a peek into the lives of the fortunate. It wasn't strange for her to see many of the President and Vice President-level offices still occupied while she was there cleaning. She knew that the men and women with tired eyes, hunched shoulders, and faces pinched in concentration, worked hard. In Ella's mind, their lives still seemed glamorous—more glamorous than hers. Although Ella was pretty sure everyone in New York City was leading a more glamorous life than she was.

Humming along to "Rockin' Around the Christmas Tree" she made her way through the offices, one by one. Along with photos and unique mementos from trips to exotic locales, this time of year the offices were also decorated for the holidays. With the music blaring in her ears, the decor really put her in the Christmas spirit.

That was, until she came upon the last and largest corner office. The size alone indicated its occupant was an important member of the company. A vast dark mahogany desk and buttery soft leather chairs were silhouetted against a wall of windows. The view of downtown Manhattan was spectacular, a million little lights dancing against the night sky as far as the eye could see. But that was it. Nothing else. No Christmas tree, garland, or tiny little twinkle lights. Nothing.

Maybe the person is Jewish, Ella thought to herself. But a closer look revealed no framed photos of a family on vacation and no photo of what might be a significant other. In fact, there were no photos at all.

What kind of person doesn't have any photos in their office? No one that Ella would want to know, that's for sure. From that point forward, Ella was going to call this office, "Scrooge's office." Once she finished cleaning Scrooge's office, she put her supplies away and with exhaustion starting to settle into her bones, she grabbed her things on her way to the elevator bank.

The numbers lit up as the elevator made its way to the 22nd floor. Ella layered her black puffer coat over her black uniform, which was starched and wrinkle-free. She put her black pompom hat on before looking down at herself. All black—she looked like she was going to a funeral. Tomorrow she would cheer herself look up a bit by wearing a brightly colored scarf.

The elevator dinged, announcing its arrival, and as soon as the doors started to open, Ella started to walk forward. Zipping up her coat to hide her somber outfit, she stepped into the elevator. Unbeknownst to her, someone else was stepping out of the elevator and was also not paying attention.

Smack! Ella and the unknown man collided.

"Oh, my goodness! I'm so sorry!" Ella put her hand to her heart, startled. "I didn't see anyone coming out," she looked up and into the light hazel eyes of a tall broad-shouldered man.

"No, excuse *me.* It's my fault; I was looking at my phone. I apologize," the stranger looked down at Ella. Their eyes held each other's gaze for the briefest of moments while Ella's pulse ticked up a notch.

"There's normally no one here at this hour," Ella's voice sounded breathy and weak.

"I know. I forgot something at my desk," the man looked over toward the main office. "What are you doing—?" His gaze swept down, and Ella saw him assess the uniform still peeking out from under her open jacket. "Oh, I see. Right, well, I'm sorry if I startled you," he stood up taller, his voice taking on an impersonal tone. "Have a good night," he flashed a quick, distracted smile and turned toward the office. He didn't wait for her to respond back.

Between college classes, her day job, and her night job which included cleaning dirty bathrooms, no help, and extra work, Ella's spirits still hadn't been crushed. But that change in the man's eyes the minute he realized she was "the help"? Well, that sent her spiraling down pity party lane.

On the long train commute back to Queens, Ella tried to get into *Restoring Christmas*, the Christmas romance novel she was reading, but she couldn't focus on the happy story. Typically, the idea of Christmas wishes, and happy endings made her feel like anything was possible during this magical time of year. But not tonight; tonight her heart felt heavy and it was all she could do to hold in the tears that were pooling in her large brown eyes.

So caught up in her own misery, when the train stopped at Forest Hills, Queens station, Ella almost missed her stop. Thankfully, the conductor's announcement of the stop somehow broke through Ella's thoughts and she jolted out of her seat, rushing to the train door. She barely squeaked out onto the station platform before the train doors closed.

Okay, Ella, the pity party is over. Out of habit, she reached under her scarf and took hold of the gold pendant that hung around her neck. Her father gave her the necklace when she turned thirteen and she had barely taken it off in the ten-plus years since. The front of the pendant was engraved with Ella's initials, and the back of the pendant was engraved with the words, *Nunca dejes de soñar*, which is Spanish for "Never stop dreaming."

Luis Martinez, Ella's father, moved to New York City from Puerto Rico when he was in his early twenties, about the age Ella was now. He came knowing very little English but picked up the language quickly. He knew New York City was going to give him and his future children the best opportunity to live out their dreams. After living in Queens for about a year, he met Ella's mother, Regina Bianchi, an Italian American born and raised in New York City. Luis and Regina fell fast in love and were quickly inseparable. Boldly approaching their families about their love for one another and their plans to marry, they prepared themselves for some backlash. Fortunately, both families accepted the couple. "At least they were both Catholic," Regina's mother had said.

Ella would repeatedly ask her father to tell the story of how her parents met. Their love story became the standard by which she measured all her encounters with men. Of the few men she had dated, not one of them had made her feel the way Luis had felt the moment he saw Regina.

She squeezed the pendant and summoned her father's memory, picturing his twinkling dark eyes that would crinkle when he smiled and the way his contagious laugh could brighten the mood in any situation. Her plan worked. A small smile spread across Ella's face as the feeling of her father's love surrounded her once again. She continued the short walk to the apartment she shared with her mother with a lighter step and an even lighter heart.

Although tomorrow was yet another day packed with classes and work at the bookstore followed, once again, by cleaning office buildings, she was ready for the challenge. Like her father always said, "Dreams don't work unless you do."

Chapter Two

The bell chimed as Ella opened the door to The Book Nook. After rushing to the subway from her class at NYU and sprinting from the subway to the bookstore, her entire body relaxed the moment she stepped inside. With books surrounding her and the scent of lavender wafting from the essential oil diffuser, the tiny shop in Midtown felt like home.

The storeowner, Marney, was fascinated by the oils and their subconscious effects on humans and animals alike. More specifically, she had a particular interest in how the change of oil from lavender to eucalyptus, etc. would affect the energy and mood of her labradoodle, Merry.

Letting her fingers skim over the tops of books stacked on every square inch of shelf and tabletop, Ella made her way to the back of the store.

"I'm here! Sorry I'm a few minutes late!" Ella called out, not wanting to startle the woman whose hearing wasn't as sharp as it once was—and that's putting it kindly. At a young seventy-three, Marney couldn't hear a subway train if it were barreling right through the front door of the store.

"I'm in the back!" Marney yelled with her back turned to the entrance just as Ella stopped to her right, allowing the loud reply to penetrate her ear drum at close proximity. Her left hand moved to cover her tender ear. With her right hand, she touched Marney's arm gently.

Marney turned toward her. "Oh, you're right here. I didn't see you there. How was class today?"

She pushed her long, gray waves of hair off her face, as was her habit, and a sleeve of bracelets jangled. Her thin, bird-like frame was softened by a brightly colored silk kimono which was topped with a stack of beaded necklaces. Sprawled lazily at her feet was Merry.

"It was great. We had to create lesson plans for a mock first semester of third grade."

"Sounds wonderful! You're going to be a great teacher someday." She turned and smiled at Ella before continuing. "Oh, look at that bright red scarf! That's a nice change from your typical sea of black."

"Thank you, I think?" Ella laughed as she put her book bag down and started to take off her scarf and jacket. Marney was always trying to get Ella to wear more color. "What can I help you with today?"

"Why don't we go work on the display at the front of the store. I want to arrange Christmas books on it and decorate with my collection of nutcrackers and some colored lights and shiny garland. I'm looking through my box of decorations, now."

"Do you know what would be great?" Ella was excited now. "We could do a whole section of children's Christmas books with a train running throughout the display!"

"That's a great idea! Are you sure you can't work here forever?" With a sad smile, Marney leaned into Ella for a quick hug.

The response from the older woman was surprising, but not. "You know I love working here, but once I get my degree, I'm hoping to get a teaching position as quickly as possible."

"Oh, I know. I know. And all those students you'll teach someday will be the luckiest children in New York City with a teacher like you."

Ella and Marney worked the rest of the afternoon setting up the two Christmas book display tables at the front of the store. Christmas music played softly in the background. Around 4 p.m., with the displays complete, Ella left to pick up two mocha lattes to celebrate.

In between customers, Marney asked, "Do you have to clean tonight or are you volunteering at the community center?"

"Cleaning tonight and volunteering tomorrow night."

"I don't know how you do it! Taking classes, working two jobs *and* volunteering with children? Where do you find the energy?" She sounded exhausted by the idea.

"This helps." Ella smiled as she lifted her coffee cup. "Hopefully, it's only for a few more weeks and then I'll graduate without any student loans. It took a little longer, but I'm glad I did it this way."

"You are one in a million, my Isabella. But I wish you would find some time to squeeze in a social life. You're so young! So beautiful! You need to let loose a little. Have some fun! This is New York City!" She did a little dance that made Ella laugh.

"Thanks, Marney." Ella took a deep breath. "I need to keep my head down and focus for the next few weeks." After a pause, Ella admitted, "But I am dreading my cleaning duties tonight."

"Why is that? Rosie giving you attitude again?"

"Always," Ella smiled. "But that's not why I'm dreading work tonight." Ella then went on to explain the collision with the stranger in the elevator and the way it made her feel.

"I'm so sorry, honey, but that man doesn't know you," Marney looked at Ella sympathetically. "Trust me when I say, *he* is missing out."

"Thanks, Marney. I can always count on you to cheer me up." Ella gave Marney's hand a gentle squeeze, and then glanced at the clock on the wall. "I should get going. I don't want to deal with Rosie's attitude if I'm late," Ella rolled her eyes.

"Wait! Come to the back with me before you leave." She grabbed Ella by the wrist and pulled her to the back room.

"Is everything okay?" Ella giggled. "You don't have to pull me. I need to go to the back to get my coat and bag anyway."

A woman on a mission, Marney searched through drawers and shelves pulling things out and moving piles around.

"What are you looking for? Can I help you find it?"

"Aha!" She turned around and a wide smile spread across her face. "Found it!" In her hand was a small, smooth light pink stone. "This is a rose quartz stone. I want you to carry it with you tonight." She tucked the small rock into Ella's jacket pocket before grabbing one of her bottles of essential oils. "Give me your wrist."

Ella knew the drill. This wasn't the first time Marney had tried to adjust her chakras. She knew it would be easier if she played along while Marney dabbed drops of oil on both of her wrists.

Ella did her best to hold in any laughter as Marney continued. "You see, rose quartz is known as the stone of unconditional love. When combined with the jasmine, it will help you attract more abundance, love, and happiness in your life. It will flush out any stagnant feelings and help vibrant energy flow through your entire body."

"Okayyyyy, not very subtle but thank you." Ella laughed. "But you know I'm going to clean offices, not going to a party, right?"

"You should always be ready. You never know what life has in store for you. It's best to be prepared." she clasped her hands together at her heart and her face lit up with hope.

Chapter Three

With a black coffee in one hand and a briefcase in the other, Wyatt Dawson expertly weaved through the throngs of people on the packed sidewalk in Midtown Manhattan. Because of the way the Christmas lights made the storefronts glow, most people loved New York City in December. Nostalgic music played in every store and restaurant and beautiful holiday décor turned the ordinary display windows into winter wonderlands.

Wyatt enjoyed December in the city as well, but his reasons were a little different. In December, people left him alone. The frigid morning forced people to keep their heads buried in their scarves. No one made eye contact or said hello; it was perfect.

He'd moved to the city because it was one of the few places he'd been where you could be surrounded by people but be totally alone. Raised in a large family with two brothers, two sisters, and a slew of cousins, Wyatt spent his childhood trying to find his own nook in the big, old house he grew up in where he could have solitude. He was a quiet child who enjoyed baseball and books; the chaos of his home was overwhelming. While the rest of his siblings stayed in their suburban Connecticut hometown and worked for the family business, Wyatt escaped to college in New York City as soon as he graduated from high school. And then he never left.

Every time Wyatt entered the law offices of Dawson & Hancock, he felt a surge of pride. During his undergraduate years at NYU and then law school at Columbia University, he worked every waking minute of every day. He sacrificed the partying at clubs and fraternities and worked to pay his own way through all the years of schooling. Once he graduated, he worked even harder, determined to start his own law firm as soon as possible.

His first job out of law school was at Specter North, a giant law firm in the city. The bigwig partners, if they noticed him at all, only teased him for being so serious or asked him to get them coffee and pick up their dry cleaning. The day he quit to start his own firm; his co-workers laughed. They warned him he would fail and come crawling back to beg for a job in six months. They clearly didn't know Wyatt Dawson very well.

Fueled by the skepticism from both his family and his former co-workers, Wyatt and his partner, Charles Hancock, built Dawson & Hancock into one of the largest and most powerful law firms in New York City in a relatively short amount of time. When David Dapper, a former co-worker from Specter North, came to him years later asking for a job, Wyatt had the chance to even the score. Based on how David had treated him in the past, he would have been justified in denying the position. However, the look of panicked desperation on David's face left Wyatt feeling pity for him. That moment with David was a crossroads, giving Wyatt an opportunity early on in his career to decide what kind of leader he wanted to be. He chose to give David the job. Fast-forward a few years and David Dapper was one of the most loyal, hard-working lawyers at the firm.

Wyatt took his time walking through the maze of cubicles, saying hello to all his employees. He wanted the office to feel like a family and for everyone who worked for him to feel appreciated and respected. It was not uncommon for him to catch an employee off guard by asking about an ailing parent or sick child. He remembered everything; his brain was a virtual computer. He knew every employee and their family members by name. In the cold, corporate world of New York City law firms, Dawson & Hancock proudly did things differently, and people talked about it. They became one of the most sought-after firms in all of Manhattan.

In his private corner office, Wyatt settled in to get some work done. After checking and responding to emails for over an hour straight, he leaned back in his soft leather chair and stretched.

"Mr. Dawson." A voice belonging to his assistant, Alice, buzzed through the intercom. "Marissa Mulvaney is here to discuss the Christmas party details with you."

"She needs to see me? I thought that was Dan's department. Or maybe even David's?"

"Ms. Mulvaney would like to speak with you specifically."

"Okay, send her in," Wyatt sighed.

He picked up his now cold coffee and took a sip. *Gross.* He pushed the button on the intercom. "Alice, would you mind getting me another cup of coffee? Please?"

Marissa knocked once on his office door but entered before Wyatt had the chance to respond. In a fitted red sheath dress and sky-high heels, she looked as flawless today as she did every day. Never a hair out of place or a crease in her dress, her attention to detail made her perfect for her Event Planning/Client Relations job at Dawson & Hancock.

"Marissa, how are you today?" Wyatt smiled as he stood to shake her hand.

"Good morning, Mr. Dawson. If you don't mind, I'd like to go over a few items regarding the office Christmas party." She motioned to a tablet in her hands.

"How many times do I need to tell you to call me Wyatt?" He smiled.

"Right, sorry. Wyatt."

"And of course, I don't mind. The party is top on my list of priorities," he clapped his hands together enthusiastically.

Marissa looked down at her tablet, unfazed by the sarcasm in Wyatt's voice. Then, matching that sarcasm, she said, "I can tell you're very excited for the Christmas season, Wyatt. Look how cheery and festive your office is!"

They both glanced around the bare office, not a strand of garland or string of twinkle lights to be found. There was no artwork, no framed photos of family members; there was absolutely nothing personal at all.

Wyatt chuckled. "Well, you got me there, Marissa. And I appreciate your sarcasm. However, I would also like you to know that although the Christmas party, and the whole holiday season in general, is not really my thing, I understand how important this event is to everyone who works here."

Marissa smiled and nodded, her blonde pin-straight hair bobbing with the movement of her head.

Wyatt returned her smile. "And *that* is why we have you. You are the event planning queen. I know you will put on a fabulous party that will be the highlight of the year for all Dawson & Hancock staff and clients."

"Thank you, Wyatt. I do plan to take the party to a whole new level this year. This event will go down in history as the most amazingly luxurious event this city has ever seen. Photos will be plastered all over the society pages. Everyone will want to work with us just for an invite to next year's party."

Wyatt stared at her; his eyes wide in surprise. "What exactly do you have planned? I was thinking laid back and fun—maybe a Christmas carol karaoke contest or an ugly—"

"*Do not* say ugly sweater contest," Marissa interrupted, her face pinched as if she had sucked on a lemon. "Didn't you receive the invitation?"

Wyatt looked around his desk that was bare aside from some files he was working on. "Ummm, I know I had it here somewhere...Why, are you not going to let me in without it?" he teased.

"Funny. No. All I meant was that the invitation sets the tone for the entire evening. This year's invitation is glamorous and elegant, exactly what the party will be like. I should know; I'm the one who designed the invitation."

Wyatt shrugged, ready to get on with more important work. "Okay, if that's what you think will make people happy then you have carte blanche. I trust you."

Marissa smiled like a kid on Christmas morning. "Thank you for your confidence, Wyatt. I truly appreciate the support. And now, the reason I'm here. Would you mind signing off on the catering bill, the musicians bill and the lighting crew bill? I have the contracts right here." She pulled out some paperwork and handed them to Wyatt.

He raised his eyebrows as he saw the costs displayed. "Wow, you're really going for it. Are you sure we need this much lighting? Maybe we could—"

"Yes, we need it. You said you trusted me, right?" Marissa interrupted again. She was not going to waver on this; that much was clear. The woman knew how to get what she wanted.

Wyatt relented. He nodded his head and signed the papers. "It is Christmas after all, right?"

"Now that's the spirit, sir. And since today is Wednesday and the party is on Sunday, we really don't have a choice at this point anyway."

"Thank you, Marissa. Now, if you don't mind, I need to get back to work. Someone needs to pay for this party," he teased.

"Of course, sir. Have you seen this morning's *Post*?" Marissa asked on her way out of the office. She was referring to the *New York Post*, one of the local newspapers.

"Um, no, not yet. Why?"

"I think you might be interested in what's on Page Six." With a mischievous smirk, Marissa glided out of the office.

As soon as Marissa was gone, Alice walked in with a cup of coffee and the day's *Post*.

"Thought you might want to read the paper while you have your coffee, sir," Alice giggled a little as she placed the coffee and paper on his desk. "And a reminder, your sister Alexa called again. That's twice in three days."

"Right," he nodded. "I forgot. I'll give her a call later. Thanks, Alice."

Wyatt took a sip from the steaming mug before picking up the newspaper. He flipped through the pages until he found the

Page Six section, which was oddly never on page six. Halfway down the page, a headline caused him to spit out his coffee.

NEW YORK CITY'S MOST ELIGIBLE BACHELOR

The resulting short caption was almost too much.

> *Wyatt Dawson, Founding Partner at Dawson & Hancock, the coolest law firm in town, has made it to the top of the list of our New York City's Most Eligible Bachelor search. He's incredibly handsome, whip-smart, and crazy successful—and somehow the man is single. I know what I want to find under my tree this Christmas—anyone else agree?*

Next to the article was a large photo of Wyatt walking down the street in a long coat while holding his briefcase. His face was serious, obviously oblivious to the photo being taken. He slammed the newspaper closed, sat back in his chair, and sighed. *Who took that photo?* This was the last thing he needed right now.

Chapter Four

Thankfully The Book Nook was only about ten blocks from the office building where Ella spent her nights cleaning. Out on the sidewalk on 48th Street, a blast of freezing air stung her cheeks. Hunching against the bitter cold, she shoved her hands into her jacket pockets. She immediately felt the rose quartz Marney had given her. As she rubbed the smooth stone between her fingers, her thoughts went again to her eccentric boss's words. Maybe she was right; maybe Ella should make more of an effort to socialize. With that in mind, she vowed that after Christmas and after her class finals were over, she would focus on meeting more people her own age.

Once inside the sleek lobby at 430 Fifth Avenue, Ella said hello to Jacob at the security desk and made her way over to the elevator bank. She pushed the thoughts of last night's experience with the man in the elevator out of her mind, choosing instead to admire the Christmas decorations that warmed up the typically sterile and impersonal space.

The elevator stopped on the 22nd floor and thankfully Ella found herself completely alone. No handsome strangers lingered. After changing into her uniform in the ladies' room, she got out her supplies before starting with the dreaded men's bathroom. Rubber gloves in place, she cleaned the sinks, scrubbing them until they shined. At some point, Rosie stuck her head in the bathroom to say hello and let Ella know she would get started on the cubicles.

Tonight, the bathrooms and offices were not in bad shape; perhaps the day had been a quiet one for the employees at Dawson & Hancock. The cleaning went by so quickly that when Rosie asked if she could leave a little early to catch her train, Ella agreed. Rosie had a family to get home to. Ella had only her mom, who was more than capable of fending for herself and didn't even bother to wait up for her anymore.

Before she knew it, she was walking into the last office that needed to be wiped down and vacuumed—Scrooge's office. Ella tried to imagine once again who might occupy an office with no photos, knick-knacks or plaques. She could see by the items in the garbage can that someone did, in fact, use the office, so what was the deal? *It must be a man,* she thought. And yes, she knew she was stereotyping, but she couldn't imagine a woman working this way. *Is he a cold-hearted workaholic with no family?*

As she continued to ponder what this man might look like, she pulled the chair out from the desk to vacuum under it and empty the trashcan. Running the vacuum over the carpet, she saw something silvery and shiny peeking out from under the trashcan. Since it was too big to vacuum up, Ella crawled under the desk to pick up whatever it was and throw it in the garbage.

Huffing as she pulled herself out from under the desk, she stood up and turned the shiny, thick card stock over. Her curiosity got the better of her and she read:

The Law Firm of Dawson & Hancock
Formally Invites You to Join Us for Our Annual
Holiday Celebration
Sunday, December 18th
The Grand Ballroom
Fifth Avenue, New York, NY
*Dinner * Cocktails * Dancing*
*Invitation to serve as your ticket for admission

Well that sounds like quite the party, Ella thought. This Sunday night she would likely be ordering takeout Chinese food and binge-watching Christmas movies. Staring at the gorgeous silver and blue shimmering invitation, she sighed and started to toss it in the garbage, but her fingers wouldn't let it go. With no rational explanation as to why, she tucked the invitation into her back pocket, finished cleaning the office, and grabbed her things to head home.

The whole train ride back to Queens, Ella daydreamed about the fancy Christmas party with women in long gorgeous gowns, crystal flutes of champagne offered on sterling silver trays, and tuxedo-clad servers passing bite-size crab cakes. The picture in her mind of the party was so real she could taste the crisp champagne.

Ding, ding. The sound of the train doors opening broke through Ella's thoughts as she popped up from her seat and scurried out the door just in time. For the second day in a row, she almost missed her stop.

The ground floor apartment Ella shared with her mom was cozy, albeit a little sparse. The furniture hadn't been updated in forever, but it was clean and comfortable. Years ago, Ella and her father painted light colors on the walls to try and brighten the space up. It helped a little but being in the shadow of the tall buildings that surrounded them, their apartment didn't let in a lot of natural light. Ella realized as she looked around, that the wall colors had begun to fade.

It was dark and quiet in the apartment; her mom had most likely gone to bed hours ago. Regina woke up early six days a week to work at a big department store on Madison Avenue named Leighton's. She worked in the back room unpacking shipments and distributing the items to the appropriate floors. Sometimes, if the staff that worked in the front were overwhelmed and falling behind, she helped set up the displays—one job she really enjoyed. In the front of the store where the customers congregated, Leighton's was luxurious and tranquil. Regina took pride in creating beautiful displays of sweaters, bedding, or housewares. Around the holidays,

Leighton's busiest time of year, she even helped with some of the front window Christmas displays.

Due to Regina's lengthy commute and Ella's late-night hours, she and her mom were like two ships passing in the night, rarely seeing each other during the week. But every Sunday they set aside time to share dinner. Together, they would prepare the meal, usually an Italian dish her mom grew up making or sometimes a traditional Puerto Rican meal if they were missing her father more than usual. Then mother and daughter would eat at the small dining table and catch each other up on what happened in their lives that week.

Tonight, as Ella shrugged off her winter coat and set her bag down on the kitchen counter, she was thankful for the solitude. Her mother would notice the shift in her mood, and she didn't want to worry her. She had always been a cheerful person, focusing on the positive things in her life: a loving mother, the college degree she was about to earn, Marney and The Book Nook, and the children she tutored once a week at the community center. She was thankful for all that she had. In her mind, her life was full. And it was Christmastime—the most wonderfully amazing time of year! So why did she feel so sad?

As she reached up to get a mug out of the cabinet for tea, something fell to the floor. Next to her feet lay the silver and blue sparkling Christmas party invitation.

That's it. That's what was making her feel like something was missing from her life. Well, she would take care of that.

Picking the invitation up off the floor, Ella marched over to the garbage can. She stepped down on the lever and the top popped open. Holding the invitation above the garbage, she paused for a moment, some part of her was still hesitating to be rid of it, but she forged on. She dropped the invitation into the garbage, letting the lid fall shut.

That's the end of that!

Twenty minutes later Ella rushed back in the kitchen, stepped on the lever that opened the lid and plucked the invitation out of the trashcan. *Just in case.*

Kate Kasch

She snuggled on the couch in her plaid flannel pajamas and ate an extremely healthy dinner consisting of popcorn and hot chocolate. Halfway through the Christmas romance movie playing on the Hallmark Channel, she fell asleep. Tomorrow would be a better day.

27

Chapter Five

The familiar ding of the door chime welcomed Ella back to The Book Nook. Next to the table where Ella and Marney had recently set up the children's Christmas book display stood a young boy with big brown eyes, and lashes that seemed too long for his tiny face. Ella smiled as she saw the wonder and excitement on the little boy's face. His eyes were glued to the toy train as it wound around the books.

After two great morning classes spent reviewing for her finals, the last two days of frustration and pity were a thing of the past. She shoved the negativity to the back of her brain. Ella was looking forward and focusing on all the positive things happening in her life. And now this little boy's sweet face lifted her spirits even higher.

Noting that Marney was busy with a customer, Ella went straight to the back room to drop her coat and bag. As she was about to hang her coat on the coat rack, she realized the hooks had gotten a makeover since last night. Faux pine garland, strands of twinkle lights that had yet to be plugged in, and multiple strings of popcorn garland were looped around the hooks. The strings of popcorn hung down in various stages of completion. Apparently, this was Marney's late-night project. She chuckled, picturing Marney in the back room singing loudly to Christmas music as she strung popcorn. A giant bowl of stale popcorn sat on the small desk, its contents spilling out onto the table and floor. *Oh, Marney. I guess we both enjoyed popcorn last night.* With no place to hang her coat, she draped it on the desk chair.

The little bookstore was busy that Thursday afternoon as the Christmas season was in full swing. There was a time when things were so dire at The Book Nook that Marney thought she would have to close the doors forever. However, somehow, she managed to keep things going through those lean years. People did so much online shopping and buying in large chain stores these days that they'd forgotten how wonderful smaller, individual stores could be. But recently there had been a resurgence in the popularity of independent bookstores. The ability to talk to an actual person and get advice on the perfect book for a five-year-old grandson or teenage daughter was priceless. To add to the charm, The Book Nook had complimentary hot apple cider in the colder months and lemonade in the warmer months. Thanks to these small touches and the unrivaled personal service, The Book Nook was thriving once again.

Ella was filled with joy after helping a young woman named Kayla find the perfect book to give to her boyfriend's sister. She hugged Kayla, wished her "good luck," and told her to check back in after she gave the gift to the sister.

"Oh, Ella, what am I going to do without you?" Marney moaned. "You make friends with all our customers, and then they all come back!"

Ella giggled at Marney's melodrama. "You'll be fine. We'll find you the perfect replacement. I won't leave you high and dry, I promise."

Marney sighed. "I'm going to get some tea. Would you like some?"

Ella took her phone out of her pocket to check the time. "Actually, I need to get going. I'm helping at the community center tonight. I'll re-shelve this stack of books and meet you in the back."

After distributing the stack of books back to their designated locations, Ella rushed to get her coat and bag.

"Is there something you forgot to tell me about?" Marney asked as soon as Ella rushed in. She was holding something behind her back.

Ella looked confused. "What are you talking about? And what are you hiding behind your back? Another stone? More essential oils?"

"I thought we were good friends, that's all. And good friends usually tell each other when something exciting has happened in their life," Marney feigned hurt feelings.

"I have no idea what you're talking about. I don't have anything exciting happening in my life, trust me."

Marney's hand emerged, holding the sparkling invitation.

"Oh, that. That's nothing. It's not even mine," Ella reached around Marney for her coat. "It must have fallen out of my coat pocket."

"If it was in your coat pocket, then it must be yours."

"No. I wish. I found it at the attorney's office I clean. I don't know why I kept it," Ella shook her head, a little embarrassed.

A wide smile lit up Marney's face and her eyes danced with excitement. "You realize what this is, right?"

"Yes. It's an invitation to a Christmas party for the company whose office I clean," Ella said flatly, already not liking where Marney was going with this.

"You having this invitation is a sign, Ella. This is a sign!" Marney waved the invitation in front of Ella's face. Ella kept shaking her head. "You have to go to this party. It's meant to be—and what's meant to be will always find a way."

Ella laughed at her friend, shaking her head again. "I found it under a desk while I was cleaning. It's not mine! It's for people that work at Dawson & Hancock."

"You work at Dawson & Hancock."

"It's for people that work *for* Dawson & Hancock," Ella said, rolling her eyes. "Trust me, it's not intended for me. It's on Sunday, today is Friday. That's two days—what would I even wear?"

A mischievous smile appeared on Marney's face. "You leave that to me."

Ella decided to walk uptown to the Manhattan Community Center. She needed the time to clear her head and be ready to tutor the young kids in her care. It was cold, but the night was still. It was that New York City wind that always got her; it took her breath away as it whipped in between the skyscrapers. Ella didn't mind the cold air, especially this time of year when the storefronts glowed with twinkle lights and Christmas décor. However, by the time she made it to the community center she was frozen to the bone. It was a much longer walk than she realized, and she was, for the first time, a few minutes late. Despite thinking about the Christmas party, the entire walk, she still had not decided whether she should go or not. Could she really pull something like that off? Wouldn't she stick out like a sore thumb? But it would be fun to get dressed up, sip champagne and listen to a live band play Christmas music.

Inside, the warmth made her numb fingers and toes tingle. As she signed in at the front desk, Ella pushed all thoughts of the Christmas invitation out of her head. She then hung up her coat in the conference room, which was used by the staff and volunteers as a coat room/meeting room.

The main recreation area, which was also an auditorium when it needed to be, was abuzz with energy. It was filled with kids of all different ages. A few kids were working on their homework, wearing noise-blocking headphones that the center provided. Most of the other kids were in groups, practicing for the big Christmas production the center planned to put on. They were performing a fun and lighter version of the Charles Dickens' classic, *A Christmas Carol*, complete with crazy costumes for the Ghosts of Christmas Past, Present and Future. Everyone that wanted a part got one, and the kids were bubbling over with excitement about the play. Opening night was only a week away!

"Ella! Ella! Come over here and help us!" A high-pitched voice yelled across the large room. The voice belonged to a sweet teenaged girl named Joana, who always wore her curly hair in a high ponytail. Her face was rarely without a smile. Ella knew she

31

wasn't supposed to pick favorites, but she couldn't help being partial to Joana.

She waved to Joana and made her way to the group of kids, who ranged in age from eight to eighteen. As Ella approached, Joana ran over and hugged her tightly around the waist.

"Hi, Joana! What are you all working on today?" Her spirits were immediately lifted by Joana's positive energy.

"We're working on the play!" Joana bounced with excitement. "I'm playing the Ghost of Christmas Future, and I'm going to have a crazy wig and wild clothes—it's going to be epic."

"Wow! You are perfect for that role! What can I help with?"

"Marcus isn't here today and he's playing the future version of Bob Cratchit. Do you think you could read his lines?"

"Of course!"

Each group was rehearsing a different scene in the play and Ella spent a few hours going around to each one. She stood in for any missing kids or played the part of enthusiastic audience member. Ella couldn't think of a better way to spend a Thursday night. Some might find it sad that a fun night out in New York City for twenty-four-year-old single Ella was hanging with a bunch of teens and pre-teens at a community center in Harlem, but Ella had always marched to the beat of her own drum.

Once the last child had left, an exhausted Ella returned to the conference room to put on her coat. Bonnie, the director of the center, came in to get her coat, too. The women said hello to each other.

"The play is going to be so great—the kids are beyond excited!" Ella told Bonnie.

"It's wonderful, isn't it? This is my favorite time of year," Bonnie said as she put on her long, black puffer coat. Black puffer coats were practically the wintertime uniform in New York City.

"Mine too! I feel lucky to be a part of this place. My house is so quiet and to be able to share Christmastime with these kids…it really makes my heart happy." Ella put her right hand over her heart, feeling emotional—perhaps too emotional. Out of the blue, Bonnie started to cry.

"Oh, my goodness, Bonnie! What is it? What's wrong? Did I say something to upset you?" Bonnie was not one to cry easily.

Bonnie took a tissue out of her pocket and dabbed at her eyes. "It's not you, Ella. I apologize for the tears." Ella waited patiently as Bonnie pulled herself together.

"Do you know why I started working here?" Bonnie asked.

Ella shook her head.

"I was an inner-city schoolteacher for many years, and I quickly realized that some of my students had nowhere to go after school. Their parents weren't home and there was no money for babysitters or after school activities. So, these kids were hanging out on the streets. They were good kids; they were out of options. I decided to investigate it—to see if there was something out there that could be a solution to the problem. And then I found the Manhattan Community Center. I immediately told my students about it and then got involved as a volunteer. Just like you are now, Ella.

"After about a year of volunteering, I felt that I was doing more good and making more of an impact here than I was in the classroom. I quit my job and became full-time staff at the center. That was about ten years ago. Whew, time flies when you're having fun," Bonnie stared off with a sad smile on her face, lost in the memory.

"Wow, Bonnie, I had no idea. I wish the world was filled with more people like you."

Bonnie shrugged, embarrassed by the compliment. Everything about her was practical. She wore khaki pants and a different color *Manhattan Community Center* polo shirt every day. Her face was devoid of any type of makeup and years of worrying about troubled youth had formed creases across her forehead and around her light blue eyes. Her gentle way and kind eyes masked the heartache she had endured when losing the battle with some kids whom she helplessly watched choose the wrong path.

She wasn't someone who talked about herself. With Bonnie it was one hundred percent about the kids, one hundred percent of the time. Her role at the center was more like that of a den mother, as she was the person the kids—especially the teenagers—went to if they needed to talk without fear of being judged. Since she didn't usually talk about her personal life, this unusual display of emotion worried Ella.

"I also feel blessed to have found the center and to be a small part of all the good work that happens here," Ella added.

Bonnie's face sagged and she ran her hand through her short graying hair. "Unfortunately, you won't be able to be a part of the center for much longer."

"What do you mean?" Ella said flatly, dread settling in the pit of her stomach.

"The center is closing."

"What? Why?" Thoughts of Joana's bouncing ponytail and wide smile filled her mind.

"We've lost our funding. It's that simple. Our rent is going up and our main sponsor that provides the bulk of our operating money didn't renew their donation. We won't be able to keep the doors open."

"That can't be! What about the kids? What will they do? Where will they go?"

Bonnie shook her head, tears filling her eyes once again.

"How much time do we have?"

"The center will close at the end of the year. So, only two more weeks."

Ella plopped down on a chair, dejected. All that work Bonnie had done over the past ten years was about to vanish into thin air. "There's got to be something we can do. We can't let this happen! This place means so much to these kids. And to me!"

Bonnie's eyes filled up again. "Unless you have a fairy godmother willing to cough up some major money, our coach turns into a pumpkin at midnight, December 31st."

Chapter Six

After staring at his computer for hours on end, Wyatt's eyes were starting to get blurry and his focus was waning. The Dawson & Hancock offices were quiet this late in the evening and the light from Wyatt's corner office was like a beacon illuminating an otherwise sea of darkened, abandoned desks. Wyatt stood up and walked over to the floor-to-ceiling windows that ran the length of his office. The city below was lit up like a million little twinkle lights against the black night sky. The sound of his desk phone ringing broke through the still silence.

"Wyatt Dawson," he said, his voice a little scratchy from the lack of use.

"I should have known the best way to get in touch with you was late at night on your office line," a familiar voice teased him. "This way, I don't have to go through your assistant, and you can't avoid me."

"Hi, Alexa." Wyatt couldn't help but smile at the sound of his older sister's voice. "I'm not avoiding you, I'm busy."

"Wyatt, we're all busy. I have three kids, a husband, and I work part-time. But you know what? I still make time for what's important in my life—like my family. Like you."

"I'm sorry, you're right. I'll do better, I promise." To change the subject he added, "How are Brad and the boys, anyway?"

"Brad and the boys are great, actually. Michael is obsessed with basketball; you should see him play! He's getting so tall. Everyone thinks he looks like you."

"Oh yeah? What do you think?"

"I think I wouldn't know because it's been so long, I forget what you look like."

"Don't be so dramatic. It hasn't been that long." He paused before continuing. "Did you tell Michael how much I liked basketball back in the day?"

"Of course, I did. But I think he'd rather hear it from you. All three of the boys miss their Uncle Wyatt."

Wyatt sighed thinking of his nephews. He really did miss them. "Please tell them I'm thinking of them and I'll try and come to a game sometime soon."

"Ha! I've heard that one before."

He rolled his eyes and paced around his office. He was starting to get annoyed.

"But that's not why I'm calling. Mom has been subtly asking around to see what your holiday plans are this year. I know you haven't been home for Christmas in a very long time, but I think it would mean the world to the family if you could be here this year."

It was hard for him to disappoint his siblings, which was why he had been avoiding Alexa's calls. He knew the conversation would be about his Christmas plans, and that it would be hard to say no. But being an attorney for as many years as he had, Wyatt could talk his way out of almost anything. Even family gatherings.

"You know it's not that simple. There's a reason why mom hasn't called and asked me directly if I'm coming home for Christmas. And although I would love to see you all...don't you remember the last time I was home for the holidays?"

Alexa let out a big sigh. "I know. But that was years ago! I think things will be different this time. Ol' Hank has gotten calmer as he's gotten older."

"Ha! Maybe you should have been the attorney—you're really good at making something false sound believable."

36

"I mean it, Wyatt! If you came home, you could see for yourself."

Now it was Wyatt's turn to sigh. It seemed every conversation he had with a family member resulted in a series of sarcastic remarks and deep sighs.

"Think about it. Please?"

Hearing Alexa's desperation on the other end of the line broke through Wyatt's defenses. "Okay. I'll think about it."

"Thank you, little brother!" And now, what else is going on in your life, Mr. Most Eligible Bachelor of New York City?" Alexa giggled. "I had no idea we had a celebrity in the Dawson family. Does the article have any truth to it, or are you dating someone special?"

"Don't even start. I have no idea who wrote that article or how it found its way into the *Post* but trust me, it's completely bogus. The only special person in my life is Alice, my lovely 65-year-old assistant. And speaking of work..."

"Okay, okay. I understand. This is the longest conversation we've had in years, so I'm going to consider myself having hit the jackpot tonight. Please think about Christmas, Wyatt. It would mean so much to all of us."

When Wyatt hung up the phone he was filled with equal parts nostalgia, love and heartache. Anytime he talked to a family member, whether it was his mom or one of his siblings—Alexa, Charlie, George, or Samantha—he was always filled with these same emotions and they were unwanted distractions. He preferred a little separation from it all. He never forgot his nieces' and nephews' birthdays though, and always sent the best gifts. Whatever the hottest new video game was, he sent it to his nephews. Or he asked Marissa to pick out the latest "it" bags for his nieces. He didn't want to be too closely involved with the day-to-day workings of his giant, complicated family. It was too messy for his neat and organized life of work and...well, more work.

Sitting back down in front of his computer, he was suddenly exhausted. He clicked on his email to check it one last time, and then he was going to call it a night. He could hear the cleaning crew working the vacuum in the distance, always a clue to the late hour. His stomach rumbled and he realized he hadn't even had dinner yet.

When he opened his email and saw the list of messages, his heart started to pound with panic. He clicked on the first message.

> *Wyatt Dawson, I hope you don't mind me emailing you. We have never met, but I saw the article in the paper about you and thought it was a sign: we are meant to be together! I think I'm your soulmate and I would love for you to take me to dinner. Or, I also heard your firm was having an extravagant Christmas party this Saturday night—perhaps I could be your date?*
> *Candi*

Wyatt scrolled down the list in his inbox and it was more of the same. There were probably fifty emails from women all over the country boldly asking him for a date or an invite to the Dawson & Hancock Christmas party. Some of the emails were so steamy and graphic, Wyatt had to immediately delete them for fear of Alice or someone from the compliance department seeing them.

First the phone call from Alexa and then all those emails; it was all too much and Wyatt could feel a headache coming on. Shutting down his computer for the night, he was now determined to find out the source of that photo that was sent to the newspaper. This invasion of his privacy would stop here.

Chapter Seven

Even the smell of eucalyptus and the sounds of Christmas music couldn't cheer Ella up today. After hearing about the community center closing, she couldn't shake the vision of Joana's large eyes and sweet giggle as she rehearsed her part in the play. Ella slogged through her classes and trudged to The Book Nook feeling like the weight of the world was on her shoulders.

"What is it, dear? Has something happened? Are you okay?" Marney asked immediately when she saw the look on Ella's face.

Slumping down in the soft wingback chair that sat in the front corner of the store, Ella groaned.

"Is it something with your classes? Or your mom?"

"No, no. It's nothing like that. The Manhattan Community Center—the one I volunteer for—is closing. They lost their funding and their rent is going up, and I feel awful. All those kids with nowhere to go! And they're all so excited about this play they're putting on in a week. They're oblivious to the fact that come midnight on December 31st, the place turns into a pumpkin. Or something like that," Ella groaned again.

"Oh my, I'm so sorry, Ella! I know how much that place and those kids mean to you. But think of it this way—it's Christmastime, the time for miracles. I'm sure it will all work out." Marney leaned down and gave Ella a warm hug.

"I hope you're right, Marney."

"I'm sure I'm right. Now, I hate to change the subject on you, but there is something pressing we need to discuss."

Ella stood up. "What is it? Something about the store? Please don't tell me bad news about the store, I don't think my heart can take it!"

"No, no, no. Nothing like that," Marney said, shaking her head. "This is exciting news! I have found a dress for you!"

Her brow furrowed in confusion. "A dress? For me? What do you mean? For what?"

"For the Christmas party—the fancy one at the law firm. You are going! And it's going to be amazing! Life changing!" The excitement emanating from Marney was palpable. Her arms were flailing around as if they had a mind of their own and she was bouncing up and down like a toddler. Ella couldn't help but giggle; she had never seen Marney this animated, and that was saying something.

"Marney, that's very sweet of you, but I don't think I'm up for a party right now. And we've been over this—that invitation is not mine. It wouldn't be right," Ella said with finality.

Marney wasn't ready to give up yet. "Can I at least show you the dress? It's unbelievable. I called an old friend in the fashion biz and—"

Ella rolled her eyes and cut Marney off mid-sentence. "No, Marney. Let's talk about something else."

Ella picked up a newspaper sitting on the little table next to where she was sitting, to further demonstrate that the subject was closed. Marney walked away, still feeling determined that this discussion was not over.

The sound of the bell chiming from the store's front door pulled Ella's attention away from the newspaper. Two young women walked in, both around Ella's age, both dressed fashionably yet professionally. It was obvious they worked in an office setting.

"Hello there, can I help you with something?" Ella asked the women as she stood up from the chair to greet them.

"We're just looking around, thank you," one of the girls said quickly, flashing a smile in Ella's direction.

"Okay. If you need anything, don't hesitate to ask," Ella replied, sitting back down. The two women, too distracted by their own conversation, didn't respond. They made their way toward the children's book section, which was near where Ella was sitting. As they approached, she couldn't help but overhear as the two talked excitedly.

"And the party is this weekend, can you believe it?" the one with the long curly hair said to the other.

"I know! I've *got* to get an invitation. *I must* be there. I have to see him in person."

"I heard that Sara from HR has been like, stalking some guy that works at Dawson & Hancock. She's being all super-friendly, trying to get invited as his plus one."

"I'm sooo jealous. I mean, if I knew anyone that worked there, man or woman, I would totally do the same thing. How is it neither of us know anyone who works there?"

"It can't be that we're going to miss *the* Christmas party of the year. Do you think it's possible to find out what the invitation looks like and try to create one ourselves?"

"I read online that they're going to be looking for that because of the article in the *Post* about Wyatt Dawson. Now zillions of women want to go to the party, so security is going to be like, crazy tight."

Ella sat frozen in her seat, her calm exterior completely hiding the swarm of emotions bubbling up inside. *They're talking about the Dawson & Hancock Christmas party! They're dying for an invitation!*

"I think I'm going to get this book on trains for my nephew. We need to get back to the office," the curly-haired woman continued as she held up a children's board book.

"Yeah, we don't need Pete all over us for being late. I swear, if he doesn't relax, he's going to have a nervous breakdown."

Thankfully, Marney had come out of the back and was at the register to help the women, because Ella was still recovering from shock. She had no idea the invitation she found was this coveted or that this party was *the* social event the Christmas season.

After the two young women finished their purchase and left the store, Ella picked up the newspaper again and went back to the article that had caught her eye earlier.

"Oh my god! Oh my god! It's *him*!" Her panicky voice cut through the now quiet store.

Marney came running over. "What is it? What's wrong?"

Ella stood up, holding the newspaper up for Marney to see. "It's him. That's the guy from the elevator!" She handed the newspaper to Marney.

"This man? It says his name is Wyatt Dawson. Wow, is he a looker or what?"

Ella snatched the paper back to take another look. Wyatt Dawson. He was incredibly handsome. His brooding expression reminded her of his light hazel eyes. Her heart began to race.

Marney snatched the paper out of Ella's hands and started to read. "'New York City's Most Eligible Bachelor,'" she mumbled as she skimmed the article. "And it seems he started that law firm Dawson & Hancock. You know, the one that's hosting the big Christmas party Sunday night? Hmmm, and he's obviously single..." Marney raised an eyebrow at Ella.

She looked straight into Marney's eyes. "Let me see the dress."

"Well, I don't have an actual dress to show you yet, but I know where we can find the perfect one!" Then: "Why do you look nervous? Don't you trust me?"

"Of course, I do! Your style is...well, your style is different than mine."

Ella's voice went up an octave at the end of the sentence; she tried to be honest about her concerns without offending Marney. It wasn't that Marney didn't have style, she dressed in a unique way—very eclectic and vibrant. She was always draped in bright fabrics, with stacks of bracelets and layers of necklaces. Patterned scarves might be tied around her head one day, her neck the following day, and her waist the day after that. In truth, Ella admired Marney's bold fashion, but it was pretty much the opposite of Ella's own style. And not what Ella had in mind for an elegant gala.

Thankfully Marney was almost impossible to offend, and she giggled at Ella's skepticism.

"You do know what I did for a living before I opened The Book Nook, right?"

Ella shook her head. "No, you've never told me."

"I was in the fashion world, and I still have quite a few connections there. It's been a while, but I can still summon the fashion gods."

"Wait, you worked in fashion before this? How have you never told me this? Did you work for a designer, a store or boutique?"

"Have you ever heard of Liana Lapierre?"

"Liana Lapierre! Of course, I've heard of Liana Lapierre— she's only the most talented, famous, French designer of all time. *You* know Liana Lapierre?" Ella stood up and practically jumped up and down with excitement. "She's the most amazing dress designer *ever*. I see her designs on all the famous actresses in my magazines!"

Marney smiled, playing coy. "Liana and I go way back. I worked with her many, many years ago when she was just starting out. She had moved to New York with big dreams and even more talent, and I was one of her first employees. We spent many late nights in her tiny studio coming up with designs," Marney's eyes glazed over as she reminisced about her younger years.

"I can't believe I didn't know this!"

"It was an exciting time, and I am happy for all her success. She is a special woman. I will tell you more about her some other time but right now, we need to get you a dress."

The two women heard the dinging of the front doorbell again. "I'll go deal with that, you find a way to contact Liana Lapierre," Ella said as she jumped out of her chair.

"Well, that's easy dear, I'll call her," Marney responded matter-of-factly.

"You can call her? Ohmigoodness, this is too much." She threw her hands up, exasperated. "I'll be right back."

She helped an older woman find some books for all her many grandchildren, which took much longer than she hoped it would. When the customer had left the store, Ella raced to the back room.

"What did I miss? Did you call her? What did she say?"

"Calm down my Isabella," Marney laughed. "It's all worked out. I know Sunday is your day off, but if you wouldn't mind coming in, I will have some options for you."

"Some options? What does that mean?"

"Trust me. You will be the belle of the ball," Marney winked.

Chapter Eight

Friday night was a cleaning night for Ella. On this Friday night, she was thankful for the work because if she had to go home straight from The Book Nook it would have left her with too much time to think. As it was, while she worked in the offices of Dawson & Hancock, her mind was racing.

Was she really going to go to this Christmas party tomorrow night? Was this even a good idea? It's not as if Wyatt Dawson would look twice at her. He would most likely be at the party with some supermodel as his date.

As these thoughts fought with her self-confidence, she was leaning toward calling the whole thing off. But then there was the matter of Marney, and the favors she had called in. And Liana Lapierre! Ella was going to get to wear a dress designed by Liana Lapierre!

Throughout the course of her cleaning she had changed her mind between going to the party and not going to the party about ten times. When the 22nd floor was almost all clean, she went to look for Rosie in the big back offices to see if she needed any help finishing up. She found Rosie in Scrooge's office.

"Hi Rosie, how's it going?"

Rosie turned around and acknowledged Ella with a nod. This was the first time she noticed how slowly Rosie was moving. Although not sure of her exact age, Ella figured Rosie to be in her late fifties, maybe even sixty years old. She had been cleaning nights for at least twenty years and Ella could see that the work was starting to take a toll on Rosie's body.

"Isn't it strange that this person—I'm assuming it's a man," Rosie said, rolling her eyes, "—that this man doesn't have anything personal in here? No artwork, no framed photos, no Christmas decorations...he must be loco." She twirled her finger in circles next to her head, the universal sign for "crazy."

"I know. I was thinking the same thing. I call this Scrooge's office," Ella said as she reached under the desk to grab the garbage can. She didn't want Rosie to have to bend down. As she was leaning under the desk, she couldn't help but remember the one thing she did find in this office: the Christmas invitation.

"Ella, are you okay? You seem flushed."

Flustered, Ella pulled the garbage can out quickly, and then yanked at the bag that lined the can. Thankfully the bag wasn't very full, since she tugged too hard and its contents scattered all around the office. Papers of all sizes were now spread all over the desk and floor.

Thrusting her hands on her hips, Rosie glared at Ella. "What has gotten into you?"

"I'm so sorry. I'll clean it all up, I promise."

"Oh, I know you will," Rosie said matter-of-factly. "But you're also going to tell me what has you all in a tizzy."

Ella stopped gathering up all the papers and sighed. "Okay, here's the situation. The other night when I was cleaning this office for you, I found something..."

Rosie's eyes grew large. "What did you find? A body? A weapon?"

She couldn't help but laugh. "Rosie, it scares me that your mind goes immediately to a dead body or a weapon!"

"I've seen a lot in my lifetime, Miss Ella." Rosie shook her head from side to side.

Ignoring Rosie's theatrics, she continued. "No. I found an invitation to this law firm's Christmas party."

Rosie was confused. "You are all flustered because you found an invitation? To a Christmas party?"

"The invitation acts as a ticket to the event. And I have it."

"You have a ticket to a Christmas party?" Rosie was still waiting for the part of the story that would cause Ella to be worried and blushing.

"Yes. And I think I'm going to go. To the party. It's Sunday night."

"Okay. Have fun. Can you clean this up first? We still need to vacuum."

Ella giggled. Once she said it to someone like Rosie, it didn't seem like such a big deal. She was going to a Christmas party. Most people went to Christmas parties! Rosie's reaction helped put things in perspective and made her feel silly for all the stress she had been feeling all day.

But Ella's sense of relief was short-lived. Later that night when she was lying in bed, sleep would not come. As she tossed and turned, her restless mind was filled with images of her showing up to the fancy party in her cleaning uniform, people mistaking her for a server, and Wyatt Dawson throwing his coat at her as if she were working the coat check. And then there was the matter of Marney. Could she really trust Marney to come up with the perfect dress? What if it didn't fit? Or it was horribly gaudy or even worse, too plain?

She spent Saturday volunteering at the Community Center and trying to study for her upcoming finals which were next week, but she found it difficult to concentrate. And she spent the evening anxiously staring at her bedroom ceiling and imagining worst-case scenarios. When her alarm sounded on Sunday morning, Ella felt as if she had only just fallen asleep. Groggy and irritable, she shoved her feet into her fuzzy slippers and went out to the kitchen to make some coffee.

"Morning, sweetheart," Ella's mom said as she poured coffee into a to-go cup.

"Morning, Mom. Off to work already?"

"Oh, you know, a Sunday during Christmas season is prime time for retail. What does your day look like?"

"I'm going to The Book Nook."

"You're working today? You usually don't work Sundays, right?"

"I'm not working. Marney's helping me with something. "

"Helping you with a school project?"

"Not exactly," Ella admitted, pouring some steaming coffee into her favorite Christmas mug. "I'm actually going to a Christmas party tonight and Marney is helping me get ready."

A smile broke out on Regina's face and she ran over and hugged her daughter tightly. "I'm thrilled you're going to a party tonight! I worry about you always working, working, working. A beautiful young girl like you ought to be having fun! Do you need anything?" Regina's petite, slight figure looked like it might burst with the excitement suddenly rushing through it.

Ella giggled. "No, Mom. Thank you, but I think I have everything I need. Marney's going to let me borrow a dress."

"Oh, wait!" Regina said as she jumped up and ran toward her bedroom. "I have the perfect thing!"

Ella laughed at how everyone seemed desperate for her to get out and socialize. Was she that much of a recluse?

Regina came out of her bedroom carrying something white and fluffy.

"What is it?" she asked, curious about what the object could be.

"It's the nicest thing I own. Isn't it gorgeous?" Regina asked, holding up the white coat for Ella to see. "It belonged to your Abuela, your father's mother. I remember the one time I saw her wear it; she looked like a movie star." Regina's eyes glazed over as she reminisced. The coat was long, with a furry collar and a belt at the waist. "Here, try it on!" She held out the coat, and Ella slid her arms through the sleeves. It was heavy, soft, and very warm. "It's cashmere. Isn't it the most beautiful winter white? Turn around, let me see you," Regina instructed.

Ella turned to face her mom as she belted the coat around her thin waist.

Regina gasped. "You look like an angel! Oh, Ella! I have such a good feeling about tonight. I hope you have a wonderful time." She wiped a tear from Ella's eye.

"Thank you, Mom! This coat is perfect. I can't believe I've never seen it before!" Ella hugged the coat around her body.

"I never got the chance to wear it very much, but I hope it will be different for you. I want you to wear it all the time. It's silly that we save our favorite things, the things that make us the happiest, for only the most special occasions. We should be making the everyday special, don't you think?"

Ella stared at her mother, so filled with overflowing gratitude and love that her eyes welled up. "Thank you, Mom. This will guarantee that tonight will be special." She wrapped her mother in a giant hug.

Once her mom left for work, she hopped in the shower, feeling light and whimsical. She blasted Christmas music and danced around her room as she dressed for the day. No matter what happened at the Christmas party later, she was going to savor every minute, because it was Christmastime in New York City and she was going to celebrate.

By the time she walked into The Book Nook, Ella was walking on air. It was as if a magical cloud surrounded her, lifting her spirits high. She had a glow about her that made her look ethereal. On her walk to the store, every passerby had smiled at her and she had smiled right back. This kind of happiness was contagious.

"Why Ella, you look stunning! That coat!" Marney swooned.

Ella twirled around for added affect. "It was my Abuela's. Isn't it amazing? My mom lent it to me."

"It is absolutely gorgeous," gushed Marney, unable to contain her excitement. "This is going to be a blast!"

Ella hung the coat up carefully. "Okay, what first? Do you have a dress for me to try on?"

"First, we need lattes—my treat. Then we wait for the team to arrive."

"The team? What do you mean, team?"

"You'll see," said Marney with a mischievous smile. "Here, take this money and go get us some lattes. By the time you get back, we should be ready!"

A mixture of fear, anxiety and excitement consumed Ella as she waited in line at the coffee shop up the block from The Book Nook. Could she really trust Marney to find her the perfect dress? And what did she mean by *team*?

As was the case whenever she was in a rush, the line for coffee moved slowly and Ella's patience was wearing thin. When her order was finally ready, she grabbed the two lattes and rushed back down the block to the bookstore. Maybe she was gone longer than she thought, because the store, which was quiet when she left, was now packed with people. She walked in slowly, trying to decipher if these people were customers or other visitors. When Ella walked by one small group of women, one of them gasped, "She's here!"

Suddenly, the bustling and chatting stopped dead, and all eyes were on Ella. This of course made Ella very uncomfortable, as she wasn't one who enjoyed being the center of attention. In fact, she absolutely loathed unnecessary attention. She stood still in her beautiful winter white coat holding the two lattes, staring back at all the unfamiliar faces that were staring at her. And then her eyes landed on someone she recognized.

"Ohmigod, Liana Lapierre!"

A tall, thin woman with light gray hair styled in a precise bob stepped forward and smiled. She wore perfectly tailored black pants that hit at her ankles and a black fitted top that was long-sleeved on the left arm and completely bare on the right arm. The top had an asymmetrical hem that flattered Liana's figure. The only spot of color in the whole outfit was her signature red lipstick. She was the definition of chic.

Liana Lapierre reached out and placed her hands on Ella's shoulders and in a French accent that sounded impossibly posh said, "Isabella Martinez, such a pleasure to meet you. Marney has told us all about you, I feel as though I know you."

Awestruck, Ella stammered out some barely coherent words that hopefully sounded like, "Nice to meet you, too."

Liana laughed, and the sound was like a rainbow. "We are going to have fun, oui?"

With a goofy smile plastered on her face, all Ella could say was, "Oui, oui!"

The group of people that were surrounding them erupted into applause and someone even let out a whistle. Marney ran up to Ella, pulled her into a hug and whispered in her ear, "This is going to be magical!"

The back room of the store was unrecognizable. The large wooden desk had been pushed against the wall. Two full-length mirrors were set up, and a rolling rack that was filled with clothes had appeared. About twenty shoe boxes were stacked up in front of it. A large vanity and chair were squeezed into the corner and was piled high with cases and cases of makeup. They had brought every hair product and hair tool imaginable, including a hair dryer, curling irons of all different sizes, and a straightening iron.

Ella's mouth dropped open in disbelief.

"I know, isn't it incredible?" Marney stood next to her and put her arm around her. "They call themselves the 'glam squad' and they know what they're doing."

"Oh, my goodness, Marney, how can I ever thank you?" She turned to face Marney.

"Have the time of your life tonight—that's all the thanks I need. Listen, I'm going to have to be in and out since I do have to take care of the store. It's a Sunday near Christmas, we'll be busy. But I'll sneak back here to check on you when I can!"

"In the meantime, we'll take good care of you," Liana Lapierre said. "Now, I'm thinking first we start with the dress! How does that sound, Isabella?"

The way Liana Lapierre said, "Isabella," immediately made Ella feel important and beautiful. The combination of Liana's voice and accent was like music.

Ella nodded her head in agreement. She was mostly concerned about finding the perfect dress. If she could find that first it would most likely lessen her anxiety.

"Angela, Donny, and Jessie—can you three start pulling dresses that you think will work with Isabella's gorgeous skin tone?"

Two women and one man scurried over to the rolling rack and started to sort through the dresses. A woman with rainbow hair, black rimmed glasses and bright lipstick took Ella's hair out of her ponytail. She ran her hands through Ella's hair and then twisted it and plopped it on top of her head. Ella stood still, silently wondering what was happening.

"This is Jackie," Liana explained, "she is the most amazing hair stylist you will ever meet. And over there," she pointed to a man with a shiny shaved head, "that is Mac. He is a miracle worker with makeup—not that you need a miracle with that smooth, golden skin."

Ella blushed from the compliment. She had never even looked at her skin that closely, and her makeup routine consisted of mascara and Chapstick.

"Isabella, would you mind coming over here?" Angela yelled from the rolling rack. "We have some dresses we'd like you to try on!"

Ella stepped behind a partition that was set up to create a little dressing area, where she found three gorgeous Liana Lapierre original dresses waiting for her. She gasped at the sight and pinched herself. Was this really happening?

The first dress she tried on was a black, simple short dress. When she stepped out from behind the screen, there were six people waiting to critique her.

"It's a great cocktail dress, but it doesn't have the 'wow factor' we're looking for," Liana said. The others nodded in agreement.

The next dress was a long, flowing winter white dress with lots of beading. It fit Ella perfectly and it made her feel like royalty. She emerged from the dressing area and received smiles and small nods from the team. Ella looked at herself in one of the mirrors and decided she really liked this dress.

Everyone turned to Liana, waiting for her response. She took her time inspecting Ella. "It's beautiful, but too bridal-like," she finally said. "Try another."

Following directions, Ella went back to try on the next option. Liana found fault with a few more dresses and Ella worried they would never find the right gown. The next dress that Angela handed her was red, which made Ella nervous. Red was a statement color. Red demanded attention and Ella wasn't sure she wanted any extra attention at the party. She put it on and could tell the fit was perfect, but she wasn't sure what it looked like until she had the chance to look in the mirror on the other side of the partition.

When she stepped out from her changing area, the room went quiet except for one gasp coming from Mac, the makeup guru. Was the silence a good thing or a bad thing?

Ella turned toward the mirror and gasped at her reflection. She couldn't believe the woman in the mirror was Ella Martinez from Queens. The dress was gorgeous. Sleeveless, with wide straps that were trimmed in velvet and a deep V-neck that plunged in the front and the back. The gown was cinched at the waist with velvet and had an A-line silhouette with a floor-sweeping hem. The skirt was full and textured. The dress color faded from dark red at the top to a lighter hue at the bottom, creating an ombre effect. It was a work of art.

"This is it. This is it!" Liana Lapierre could not contain her excitement. "It's as if this dress was designed especially for you, Isabella."

Everyone agreed and fawned over Ella with compliments. Even with her hair up in a messy bun, with no makeup or shoes, Ella already felt like a different person.

"Okay, that took a little bit longer than we thought to find the perfect dress, but we did it! And it was worth the wait. But now, we need to move things along. Angela, Donny and Jessie—find her some shoe options. And then Jackie, you're up. I think she should wear her hair down; what were you thinking?"

"I was thinking the same thing. She has nice, thick hair. I can do something really special with it."

After trying on a few pairs of shoes, Ella and Liana decided on a pair of sparkly, strappy heels. There was a little sequin clutch to match. With a robe on to protect the dress, Ella sat down and let Jackie get started on her hair. She tried to relax and enjoy the pampering, but her heart was pounding, and her mind was racing with anticipation.

After her hair was finished, which took longer than Ella would normally spend on her hair in a month, Mac came over to work his makeup magic. Mac kept Ella facing him, with her back to the mirror so she couldn't see what he was doing. He wanted the big dramatic reveal when he was finished. At some point sandwiches and snacks were brought in for everyone, and Ella did her best to eat but nerves had her stomach in knots.

Marney came rushing to the back of the store while Mac was working on Ella's makeup. "Whew! The store is unbelievably busy today! I haven't had a minute to check in back here and I'm dying with curiosity! How is everything going? We are getting close to the start of the party—are you almost done glamming up?"

"We're almost done, Marney, no worries. Mac is going to finish my makeup and then the makeover will be complete!"

"Wait until you see her dress," Mac gushed.

"Ah! I can't take it! I want to see! How much longer, Mac?"

"Give me about ten more minutes," Mac smiled.

"Ten minutes? I don't think I can wait ten minutes!"

Ella and Mac laughed. The sound of the ding from the front door had Marney rushing back to the front of the store. Only ten more minutes and Ella would be done. That meant it was almost time to go to the party and Ella's pulse quickened with anxiety.

Before she knew it, Mac was asking her if she was ready to see herself. As she held her breath and squeezed her eyes shut, Mac spun the chair around, so she was facing the mirror.

"Okay, now open your eyes," Mac whispered. Despite the softness of his voice, everyone in the room seemed to stop what they were doing and look over at Ella.

With one more deep breath, Ella slowly opened her eyes.

Her jaw dropped open in shock. She turned her head from side to side and leaned in toward the mirror to get a closer look. During the makeover, Ella had feared she wouldn't look like herself. She worried the transformation would make her feel like a phony. But this makeup only enhanced her natural beauty. Eyeshadow in shades of gold and layers of black mascara made her eyes looked large and bright. A blend of bronzer and blush had her skin glowing and defined her high cheekbones. Her lips were painted the exact red of the dress she wore.

Waves of dark hair fell down her back, with a deep side part that reminded Ella of the glamorous actresses of old Hollywood. If Ella had seen a woman walking down the street that looked like she did right now, she would assume the woman was a famous actress or singer. The soon-to-be grade-school teacher was still there underneath the gloss, but now her sophistication and elegance took center stage.

No one had spoken yet. All members of Liana Lapierre's glam squad were ogling Ella with giant smiles, clearly proud of their work and in awe of her beauty. Ella swiveled the chair around to face the crew, stood up, and took off the robe that had been covering her gown.

Liana Lapierre broke the silence first. "Bippity, boppity, boo!" she quoted the fairy godmother from "Cinderella." As she said the words, she dipped her hand at Ella as if she were brandishing a wand.

At that exact moment Marney came bursting through the back-room door. In a rather theatrical reaction, she stopped dead in her tracks, smacked her right hand to her heart, and yelled some indecipherable sounds that were something between a squeal and a cry.

"Yes, that's it," Marney said, finally finding some actual English words. "Cinderella. That's you tonight, Isabella. You have been slaving away with school and work and volunteering. You've had no sleep and no fun, but tonight the princess that has been hiding inside you will be revealed to the world."

Laughing at Marney's melodrama, Ella blushed at all the fuss being made over her. "All this talk of princesses and Cinderella has my nerves in a flurry. I don't want to put too much expectation on tonight's event—it is just a Christmas party after all."

"What is it your father always said about dreams?" Marney walked over and gently placed her hands on Ella's shoulders.

"Dreams don't work unless you do?" she asked, confused how that saying might apply to this situation.

Marney shook her head, "No, no, not that one. The one in Spanish."

"*Nunca dejes de sonar*. Never stop dreaming."

"Yes!" Marney's face lit up, "Yes! Never stop dreaming. Believe that tonight will be magical, and it will!"

"What about, 'Expectation is the root of all heartache?'" Ella countered.

"Whoever said that clearly had no idea what they were talking about."

"It was Shakespeare, Marney. Shakespeare!"

"Shakespeare also wrote nothing but tragedies. I prefer Cinder-*ella*!" Marney said, emphasizing the second half of the name.

Ella and the rest of the glam squad couldn't help but laugh at Marney's unfaltering positivity.

"Okay, people," Liana clapped her hands together, "I'm looking at our Isabella and I feel like she's missing something. What is it?"

"Missing something? She's perfect!" Jackie squealed.

"I know what's missing," Marney grinned. "Jewelry!"

"Oui! That's it! She needs some bling, maybe earrings and a bracelet. That thin necklace you have on actually works well, you should keep that," Liana was talking a mile a minute.

"Angela, Donny, and Jessie—what did we bring for accessories?"

The three stylists looked at each other and then back at Liana sheepishly.

"What is it? Did you not bring any jewelry? She's going to a gala and you brought no bling?"

"Wait!" Marney cried, jumping slightly. "I have just the thing!" She ran toward the desk which was currently covered in boxes, dresses, jackets and handbags and started throwing things all over the place. Everyone watched her, curious to see what Marney, who was covered in layers of costume jewelry, would come up with.

"Aha! I've found it!" She pulled out a black felt box and carefully lifted the lid. "The Crown Jewels," she batted her eyes and held out the box.

"I'm not sure I need anything else," Ella said hesitantly. She had always preferred an understated look. Marney, on the other hand, didn't believe in too many accessories. She pulled out a sparkling pair of chandelier earrings and a matching cuff bracelet, and for the millionth time, Ella gasped.

Mac popped a bottle of champagne, and they all clinked glasses in a congratulatory toast. She was hoping the champagne would relax her, which was most likely the reason Marney bought it in the first place, but an entire bottle of champagne wouldn't have calmed Ella's nerves that night.

After a few group photos with the squad and Marney, Ella couldn't believe it was time to go. Her stomach was a tangled knot of anxiety as she slipped on the white cashmere coat. She tucked her phone, the red lipstick that Mac gave her, some cash, and the now-famous blue and silver Christmas invitation into the sequined clutch.

"How do I get all of this back to you?" Ella asked as she kissed Liana on each cheek.

"Bring it back to Marney at the store tomorrow and we'll arrange it. But don't be thinking about the end yet, savor every moment of right now, Isabella."

After one last good-bye, Ella walked out of The Book Nook and onto the busy New York City sidewalk. Wearing a dress worth more than she made in a month and on her way to an elegant party, she felt as if she had transcended her working-class life and joined the exclusive "other half." Full of a confidence she had never before felt in her twenty-four years, she was ready to play the part. And as if right on cue, a horse-drawn carriage pulled up in front of the store.

Completely caught by surprise, she turned back to look through the glass door at Marney and Liana, who were watching her with knowing smiles. Marney poked her head out. "A princess can't show up to the ball in a yellow cab!" she cried.

Ella put her hands to her heart and mouthed the words, "Thank you," before blowing Marney a kiss. She turned to the street and with the help of the coach driver, stepped up into the carriage thinking, *hopefully this doesn't turn into a pumpkin at midnight!*

Chapter Nine

The ride from The Book Nook to the Dawson & Hancock building was spectacular. It was a cold, clear night and Ella watched in awe as the city slipped by slowly. This was the first time in her life that she was able to see the city at Christmastime in slow motion. Normally, she was either walking along a crowded sidewalk with her head down braced against the cold, on a subway under the city, or speeding by in a cab. On this glorious winter night, Ella gazed at twinkling Christmas lights, bustling people excited for their Saturday night, and large storefront windows elaborately decorated with Christmas and winter-themed scenes.

As her sparkly Jimmy Choo stiletto hit the pavement in front of 430 Fifth Avenue, the flurry of nerves in her belly dissolved. She emerged from the carriage as Isabella—confident and standing tall and proud. Sometime later she could analyze why clothing and makeup drastically improved her self-esteem, but tonight as onlookers on the sidewalk stopped to stare at the dark-haired beauty in the gorgeous white coat stepping out of a horse-drawn carriage, she decided she was going to own this alter-ego.

The ballroom was on the top floor of the building. Ella walked slowly across the lobby toward the elevator bank. Out of habit, she was about to say hello to Jacob, the night security guard she knew well. However, sensing no recognition in his eyes, she held back. Instead she strolled right up to him and said politely, "Good evening."

"Evening," Jacob replied to her. "I assume you're going to the Dawson & Hancock Christmas party?"

"Yes, I am. It's on the top floor?"

"Yes, ma'am."

Ma'am? This was the same guy she said hello to almost every night for over a year and he didn't recognize her!

"Do you have the Christmas invitation for admission?"

She reached in her clutch and showed Jacob the invitation.

"Thank you, ma'am. You can go right up. It's the 44th floor—the penthouse level. Enjoy your evening."

The elevator doors opened on the top floor and Ella inhaled deeply with anticipation. She was greeted by a server offering flutes of chilled champagne, who was standing in front of thick, navy-blue velvet curtains that separated the entryway from the rest of the ballroom. She smiled at the server as she accepted a glass of bubbly. Stepping through the heavy curtains was like entering a new world. A world where the people glowed as bright as the enormous crystal chandeliers.

A million twinkle lights dangling from the ceiling transformed the top floor of the office building into a Christmas wonderland. A sea of high round tables with glittering tablecloths and topped with tall white floral centerpieces sparkled under the lights. In the back of the large rectangular space, a stage draped in silver and flanked by frosted Christmas trees held a full band playing soft Christmas music. The instrumental music, along with the gentle chatter of the guests and the clinking of glasses, created a whimsical background melody.

A server in a tuxedo sashayed over to Ella and held out a tray displaying what she assumed were mini crab cakes. Although the crab cakes looked delicious, with her stomach aflutter with tension and excitement, she declined the food and opted for another sip of her champagne instead. She sidled up to one of the tall tables, taking in her surroundings. There must have been ten Christmas trees, each decorated from top to bottom in crystal and silver ornaments and wrapped in blue and silver ribbon. Before the night was over, Ella was hoping to sneak a photo of the beautiful trees to show her mom later.

Enjoying the music and the champagne, Ella watched the other guests with fascination. The women wore floor-length luxurious gowns, and shimmering jewels hung from their ears or around their necks. Their hair was swept up in complicated twists and braids. The men were all in tuxedos which made it hard to distinguish one from the other. The continual chatter amongst the guests suggested that most of the people in attendance knew each other. No doubt they all were a part of the same social circle—one that Ella was certain she would never be privy to herself. One woman, with a cobalt blue fitted dress that flared at the bottom like a mermaid tail, seemed to be making the rounds, schmoozing with every person in attendance. She had chin-length blonde hair and oozed confidence, commanding attention from everyone she encountered.

The blonde woman's self-assuredness inspired Ella. Right then and there she decided that tonight she would not think about tomorrow's reality. She pushed everything to the back of her mind—exams, the bookstore, the community center, and cleaning bathrooms. Tonight, in her Liana Lapierre gown with her hair cascading down her back, she was Isabella Martinez, and she was going to live in this moment.

Suddenly, the quiet murmuring of the crowd grew louder. Ella could sense a building excitement as a group of women turned to each other, giggling and squealing. Ella looked on with curiosity. A dark-haired man walked through the navy velvet curtains and with one glance Ella's breath caught in her throat. It was him. Wyatt Dawson.

It wasn't only Ella's heart that was palpitating at the sight of the handsome attorney. Every woman in the room was swooning and vying for his attention. Although every male guest wore a tuxedo, Wyatt stood out above the rest. His broad shoulders, statuesque build and supreme air of confidence were magnetic. Ella could not stop staring.

Men and women alike seemed to wait with bated breath as Wyatt made his way across the crowded room, expertly weaving through the tables saying hello to everyone he passed. She could not pry her eyes off him, appreciating how he addressed each person by first name. As he shook a short, stout older man's hand he happened to glance up at Ella. Their eyes locked with an intensity neither had ever felt before.

She felt like the background noise seemed to fade away and every other person in the room became a blur against the sharpness of Wyatt's piercing light eyes. She gripped the table's edge for fear of her knees buckling beneath her. With his eyes never straying from hers, he glided to the back table where she stood. Her heart hammered in her chest.

"Hi," he said slowly. His voice was deep and smooth, and he looked at Ella with an almost confused expression.

"Hi." The word came out like a whisper.

He held his hand out for her to shake. "I'm Wyatt, I don't think we've met."

Ella thought briefly of the episode in the elevator when she had just finished cleaning his office, but she quickly pushed that out of her mind. "Isabella." She reached out and shook his hand. The feel of his hand around hers was like an electric shock, and they both stared at each other, startled by the jolt.

"Isabella. How is it we've never met before?"

The way her name sounded coming out of his mouth made her tingle all over and goose bumps ran up her neck.

Coyly shrugging as if to suggest it was some strange lack of coincidence that the two had never crossed paths, Ella said, "I don't work for Dawson & Hancock."

"Oh, I see. You're here as someone's guest?" He tried to hide his disappointment. *She must be someone's date.*

Before Ella could answer, the beautiful blonde in the cobalt blue dress rushed up to him. "Wyatt, could I speak with you?" She turned to Ella and smiled politely. Sensing she had interrupted an intense exchange, she quickly said, "It will only take a moment."

Wyatt looked to Ella for approval. Surprised by the thoughtful gesture, all she could muster was a slow nod of her head. Relieved, he said, "I will be right back. Don't move."

Stepping aside to speak with Marissa, Wyatt's typical cool and calm demeanor had turned impatient and brusque. "What's up? Is something wrong?"

"No, no, I apologize for pulling you away from that gorgeous young woman. And that dress! Is that a Liana Lapierre?"

Wyatt assumed that was a rhetorical question, since he obviously had no idea who designed Isabella's dress.

Marissa continued, not waiting for a response. "I can see that you are eager to return to her."

Wyatt's only response was to wave his hand in a circular motion, suggesting she quickly continue with whatever it was she needed from him.

"I'm wondering when you would like to say something to the guests? I think now is better, but you can of course do it closer to the end of the night."

"Let's do it now," he said abruptly, glancing back at Ella. He wasn't sure why, but he had a strange feeling that this Isabella woman might be a figment of his imagination—that she might disappear at any moment, never to be seen again. He was not willing to risk that. He wanted to get the speech over with and spend the rest of the night with her.

"Oh, okay. We can do that." Marissa tried to disguise her surprise at Wyatt's eagerness to get back to the woman in red. "I'll let the band know now. Come over whenever you're ready."

Nodding once, Wyatt turned and walked briskly back over to Isabella, who thankfully had not left her spot at the back table. As soon as their eyes met again, both their faces lit up with bold, unabashed smiles.

"Hi, again," Wyatt said, continuing to smile.

"Hi," Isabella said shyly.

"I have some business to attend to, please don't leave. Can you stay right here? Don't leave," he repeated.

She laughed and nodded her head. He put his hand gently on top of hers and Ella's skin ignited at the touch. With one last intense look into each other's eyes, Wyatt turned and quickly walked toward the stage. The band was playing a jazzy version of "Let it Snow."

Ella watched Wyatt walk away and took another sip of her champagne, finishing the remnants in the glass. She needed to slow down her pounding heart. It was like they had met before, and technically of course they had, but not really; not like this. This was unlike anything Ella had ever experienced. The thoughts racing through her mind were interrupted by the sound of Wyatt's voice through the speakers. She was so caught up in her own feelings she hadn't noticed the music had stopped. Glancing up at the stage she saw Wyatt at the microphone.

"Welcome, everyone! Thank you for coming tonight to the Dawson & Hancock annual Christmas party. And what a party!" Wyatt exclaimed to the cheers and applause of the crowd.

"I would first like to thank Marissa Mulvaney who spent countless hours—and lots and lots of the firm's money—planning this exquisite event."

Now the crowd was laughing, and the beautiful woman in the blue dress was nodding and smiling as those around her patted her on the back.

Ella then realized why it seemed everyone knew who the blonde was – she was the one what had planned the whole event.

"I also want to thank all of you," Wyatt continued. "Without the hard work and dedication of everyone who works at this firm — from the partners to the cleaning crew and everyone in between — Dawson & Hancock would not be where it is today."

The mention of the cleaning crew had Ella sucking in her breath and a slight panic enveloped her. *Does he know?* Ella tried to slow her breath. *You're being irrational. He doesn't know who you are.*

"Back in my law school days, I was one hundred percent focused on learning everything I could about the law and how to make it work for the people who needed it most. I cut out all distractions and focused totally on my studies. No fun, all work. I'm sure most of you find that hard to believe." He smiled as all his employees laughed at his sarcasm.

"When Charles and I started this firm years ago," Wyatt said, "we could only dream about being able to help as many people as we now do. It is a powerful thing to have influence over justice being served. To be able to help the helpless and hold the guilty accountable. I am unbelievably proud of the work we do and am excited for the future. Because with people like you lifting us up, we will all rise together."

Wow. Ella was amazed by what a talented public speaker he was. It was no wonder his firm was such a huge success, with someone so charismatic and inspiring at the helm.

"And now, to show my appreciation for the long hours each and every one of you puts in here, I have a little surprise for you all."

At that moment a shower of silver and blue confetti dropped from the ceiling. The band broke out into a cheery rendition of "We Wish You A Merry Christmas," and a team of servers flooded the room, each holding a large tray. The trays were filled with small silver-wrapped boxes tied with shiny blue bows. Much to the guests' delight, the boxes were handed out to everyone in attendance.

The previously reserved party exploded in celebration. The dance floor in front of the band quickly filled with dancers and the champagne waterfall towers were surrounded by guests eager to refill their glasses. Ella smiled as she watched the contagious energy and joy of the partygoers envelop her.

And then he was there. Standing right in front of her, his expression a tangle of surprise and expectation.

"Would you like to dance, Isabella?"

Ella was relieved the band had slowed the music down as couples swayed all around them on the dance floor. Wyatt pulled her close and she inhaled his cologne, which was a heady mixture of cinnamon and citrus. Her body relaxed against him as his right hand fell to her lower back. His other hand gently clasped hers and despite the swarm of butterflies fluttering in her stomach, it felt right. Being together with him felt natural.

"Based on this party, I get the feeling you really like Christmas?" Ella asked, looking up at Wyatt.

"If I'm being honest, I don't do much to celebrate Christmas. Members of my staff put this party together. I just show up."

"Really? Well, you had me fooled. Do you not have a lot of family?"

He laughed but there was no joy behind it. "I have a giant family. I'm one of five kids."

"You're lucky! I've always dreamed about having a big family."

"Trust me, it's not all it's cracked up to be." Wyatt's face clouded over. "Do you have any siblings?" He seemed anxious to get the focus off his family.

"No, I'm an only child. It's just me and mom. Now don't get me wrong, I'm thankful for my mom; we are very close. I guess there's something about the holidays that has me wishing for a house filled with aunts, uncles, siblings, nieces and nephews. You don't agree?"

Wyatt looked thoughtful for a minute. "A long time ago I gave up on the idea of a perfect Christmas. My family is...well, my family is complicated."

Ella nodded as they danced slowly in a comfortable silence.

"It's you and your mom, then? What about your father?"

"My father passed away a few years ago."

"I'm sorry. That must be hard, especially around the holidays."

Ella nodded. "But I've got my mom and my co-workers and the kids at the community center," she stopped herself, not wanting to reveal too much about her real life. She looked around the room before continuing. "It looks like the music has stopped," she said with a smile. The two had been so caught up in their conversation it was as if they were the only two in the room. Now, as they glanced around, they found themselves alone on the dance floor.

"I think the band is taking a break," Wyatt said, looking back down at her. "I have an idea," he said, smiling. "I want to show you something." Wyatt grabbed Ella's hand and led her through the crowd of people to the back of the room. He pushed aside a few drapes, looking for something. Ella looked on with curiosity. "What are you looking for?"

"You'll see. Give me a second." Wyatt reached back behind one of the curtains and pushed hard, his whole arm disappearing behind the fabric. He turned back toward Ella with a wicked smile and gently pulled her through the curtain with him.

Ella held Wyatt's hand tightly as he pulled her along. There was something intimate about trusting him to guide her to some unknown place, and the strong sense of connection overwhelmed her. It felt like she had known him forever.

A burst of cold air shocked Ella's skin but the dip in temperature was worth it once she realized where they were. They were on the rooftop deck of the building and the city blazed below like a million strands of twinkle lights.

"It's breathtaking," Ella sighed, hugging herself to stay warm.

"I'm sorry, I know it's freezing out here. Take my jacket," Wyatt took off his tuxedo jacket and draped it over Ella's shoulders.

"Why didn't you keep this deck open to the party?" Ella asked as she tugged Wyatt's jacket tighter around her body.

"Marissa thought it would be too cold. And judging by how much you're shivering, it looks like she was right," Wyatt laughed. "Are you okay? Do you want to go back inside?"

Ella shook her head. "I love looking down at the city, it's mesmerizing. Like watching the flames of a fire dance in a fireplace."

Wyatt nodded his head in agreement. "It never gets old for me, either." He moved closer to her. Their arms were now touching as they looked over the edge of the roof deck wall. "Can I tell you a secret?"

Ella looked up at him and nodded.

"I spent most of last year's Christmas party out here, too." He glanced sideways at Ella, waiting for her reaction.

"What? Why would you do that? A gorgeous party for your company, filled with people who are dying to be around you, and you spent it out here? Were you alone?" Ella was suddenly worried he was admitting to spending last year's party with another woman.

"I was alone," he smiled. "I don't mind my own company. All those people, all that small talk—it's really not my thing."

"Well you do a good job of faking it," Ella laughed. "You looked so calm and comfortable with all the attention in there."

"I do it for the employees. They work hard, and I'm very grateful for them. I meant everything I said in my speech. All of that," he waved his hand back at the room, "all of that is for them. I go because I have to." He turned until his whole body was facing her. "I've never been more thankful for this party than I am right now. If not for the party, I would never have met you, Isabella."

Ella turned toward him and their eyes locked. She shivered once again, but she was not sure if it was due to the December air or the storm of emotions roiling under her skin.

"You're still cold." Wyatt was concerned and started to look around the deck. Suddenly his face lit up. "Ah ha! I've got it!" In a few long strides he was across the deck and inspecting what looked like a tall pole. "It's an outdoor heater! Let me figure out how to turn it on." Wyatt's brow furrowed as he searched the heater for an 'on' switch. Ella took the opportunity to study his face; the straight cut of his jaw, his smooth olive skin, and his deep-set light hazel eyes. Was this night really happening? Was she really dressed in a Liana Lapierre gown on the rooftop of a skyscraper on Fifth Avenue with a handsome, successful, thoughtful man? If only this night would never end.

"Got it!" Wyatt proclaimed as the heater buzzed to life, immediately giving off a deep red glow and a steadily growing wave of heat. Ella rushed over toward the warmth and smiled up at him.

"My god, you look beautiful in this light." He ran his thumb down her cheek.

Ella looked down, embarrassed by the compliment.

"Tell me about your father." Wyatt didn't take his eyes off her as he pulled two patio chairs closer and offered her a seat.

Sitting down was a welcome relief, since the sky-high stilettos she had on were not exactly comfortable. She took her time thinking about how to best describe her father and Wyatt waited patiently, studying her face in silence.

"When I think about my father, which I do every day, I think about his smile." Ella smiled at the thought. "He was a very positive person, and nothing could get him down. He had moved to New York City from Puerto Rico, filled with hope by the unlimited possibilities and opportunities. He truly believed America was the greatest country in the world."

"He sounds like an amazing man," Wyatt said softly.

She nodded. "He really was. He wanted me to dream big and do something important. He would say to me, *nunca dejas de sonar*, which means 'never stop dreaming.' He had such big expectations for me, I hope I don't disappoint him."

"What do you think he wanted for you? Because I've known you for," Wyatt looked at his watch, "a couple of hours, and I can already tell you that your father would be proud of you."

Ella giggled. "I know he wanted me to finish college, get a job doing something that I loved, start a family...you know, the American dream."

"Do you know what you want to be when you grow up?" Wyatt teased. "What's your dream job?"

"I want to be a teacher," Ella said definitively. He nodded and looked at her as if every word she spoke was the most important thing he'd ever heard. "When I was in the sixth grade," she continued, "I had the most amazing teacher, Mrs. Wade. She made me feel special and smart and inspired. She instilled in me a love of reading, which I will forever be grateful for. Even now, when I inhale the woody smell of books, which is quite often since I work at a bookstore, I think of Mrs. Wade."

"You're going to school to become a teacher and you're working at a bookstore. Did you say you also volunteer at a community center?"

"Yeah, the kids are great. I feel like I can make such a difference there. Right now, they're planning a Christmas play, and it's the sweetest thing I've ever seen. When I was growing up, I always loved going to the community center near where I lived. I think they're important for kids who have nowhere else to go after school. I'm sorry, I'm rambling!" Ella giggled nervously. "I don't know why I can't stop talking about myself, that's really not like me!"

Wyatt laughed. "Don't apologize! I'm fascinated. You're not like anyone I've ever met before." She was thankful for the dark cover of night, since she was pretty sure her face was as red as her dress. "Tell me this, Isabella. With school, your job and volunteering, how do you have time for a social life?"

"I don't," Ella said with a laugh.

"I find that very hard to believe."

"I heard your speech; I'm pretty sure you're the same way. All work, no play. For now, at least."

"I guess we have a lot in common," Wyatt's face lit up with delight.

"I'm pretty sure that's the *only* thing we have in common."

"Why would you say that?" he asked.

"Never mind," she sighed, shaking her head. "Enough about me, tell me about your big giant family!" She noticed Wyatt's face cloud over at the mention of his family. "What is it? What's wrong?"

Wyatt shook his head. "It's nothing. It's my family, they're well…"

"Complicated," Ella repeated what he had told her earlier.

"Yes. Complicated," he said, smiling. "My family runs a chain of sporting goods stores, and all my brothers and sisters work for the company."

"And you didn't want to work for the family business?" Ella asked.

"I didn't. And I still don't."

"And that upset some family members?"

"A little bit. I think they all wish I worked for the company, but that's not the main issue. The main issue has to do with my current profession."

"They don't like that you're an attorney?" Ella was confused. "Don't most parents want their kids to be doctors and lawyers?"

"You would think so," Wyatt said, "but my dad hates lawyers. I'm talking, *really* hates lawyers."

"I don't understand."

"A customer slipped on a wet floor in one of our stores. It seems another customer had spilled their coffee, and before any of the employees could mop it up, this other customer slipped in it and got a minor injury. This person, obviously of the litigious sort, sued the company. The lawyers representing the injured party were, let's just say, not good people. They saw the size of the company and really went after it, asking for an obscene amount of money. My father, being slightly naïve, didn't believe that any court would rule in this woman's favor. To make a very long story short, my family company lost the court case, and had to pay this woman a lot of money."

"And ever since then your father has hated lawyers." Wyatt nodded his head and now Ella understood. "But you're not like those lawyers, right?" She asked.

"Of course not. I became a lawyer *because* of what happened to my father. I became a lawyer to protect people from being sued for no reason. I want to fight against these dishonest lawyers—to level the playing field."

"And your father?"

"When I told him I was going to law school, my father saw it as a personal insult. We got in a huge fight and I haven't been home for Christmas since."

"You haven't been with your family at Christmas since you were in law school?" She was shocked.

"Nope." Wyatt shook his head. "I tried one time a few years ago, and it was a total disaster. In order to avoid ruining Christmas for my entire family, I stay here in the city."

"That must be really hard. I'm sorry," Ella put her hand on top of Wyatt's and squeezed. "Whether he shows it or not, I'm sure it's hard for your father, too. He must miss you."

"He's got plenty of other family to keep him busy. I'm sure I'm not even on his radar."

"But you're his son, and he's your father," Ella paused for a moment, not wanting to say anything to upset him. "All I'm saying is, don't let stubbornness or pride get in the way of you spending time with your family. Family is everything!"

He considered her words. "You need to understand, my family is different. We don't think the same way you and your family think. We're really great at holding grudges."

Ella thought about that for a minute. "Nope. I don't believe you."

Wyatt's eyes widened in surprise. "What do you mean you don't believe me?" He was not used to anyone speaking so bluntly to him.

"I don't believe that family isn't a top priority for you. I think you need to be the one to reach out to your father. You're already the rogue family member, the one marching to the beat of his own drum. You've already been labeled the wildcard who does things differently, so do *this* differently than your dad would do it. Make the effort. I don't think you'll regret it. But you might regret losing any more time with your family than you've already lost."

Sitting across from this miraculous woman, Wyatt couldn't believe what he was hearing. His mouth hung open in astonishment. "Who are you?" he whispered, his eyes not leaving hers. Throughout the course of their conversation huddled under the patio heater, Wyatt and Ella had leaned in closer and closer toward each other. They were now mere inches from each other's faces and Wyatt, driven by a desire he had never felt before, leaned in even more. His heart raced at the thought of his lips touching hers.

"Wyatt! Wyatt, are you out here?" A woman's voice broke through Wyatt's trance. Marissa came rushing out onto the deck, hugging herself against the cold. "Wyatt, there you are! Thank god I found you. I've been looking for you everywhere!" Marissa stopped herself from running over to him when she saw he was sitting with that gorgeous woman in red.

Wyatt reluctantly stood. "What can I help you with, Marissa?"

"Would you mind coming back to the party? Dinner is being served and people are looking around for you. I don't want the employees to think you left."

Expecting him to nod and follow her back inside, Marissa was surprised to see him hesitate. It was not a shock to see him chatting with a beautiful woman, or a gaggle of beautiful women, for that matter. But the look on his face as he turned back to the dark-haired woman in red was something she had never seen before. Was Wyatt Dawson asking this woman for *permission* to leave her side?

As Marissa tried to keep her jaw from dropping to her chest, she watched Wyatt turn to this mysterious woman, who was wearing his tuxedo jacket, and whisper something into her ear. Acting on pure instinct along with her experience from many years spent in the cutthroat world of public relations in New York City, Marissa subtly pulled her phone out of her clutch and snapped a few quick photos of Wyatt and his new friend. She slipped the phone back into her bag just as he was turning back toward her, and the three of them marched back into the party with Marissa leading the way.

Once back inside, the warmth and noise of the ballroom provided a stark contrast to the cool and peaceful rooftop deck. Although she was cold outside, Ella would have stayed out there all night. The second Wyatt was seen returning, a crowd of people swarmed him. Each one yelled his name and held up their phone for a selfie request. Her heart sank as she watched him get swallowed up in the crowd and she realized that she may never see him again.

The round dinner tables matched the high-top tables at the entrance to the party. Silver tablecloths shimmered under the lights, and tall, white floral arrangements served as centerpieces. Blue and white linens lined each guest's place setting. A quick scan of the tables, and Ella realized most of the tables were full. At the back of the room, she found a few empty seats.

"Is this seat taken?" She motioned to an empty chair next to an older couple sitting together at an otherwise empty table. The gentleman shook his head.

Ella sat down, her seat in the back giving her a view of the room. The atmosphere was jovial as guests talked, laughed and drank. Minutes later a train of servers appeared holding large silver trays. Plates of salad were placed in front of every seated guest. Ella looked down at the beautiful plate, admiring how slices of thin cucumbers were artfully wrapped around the salad, creating a bowl-like vessel. With her fork she toyed with the greens, but she couldn't stomach eating anything. The separation from Wyatt had dampened her spirits and she longed to be near him again.

"Excuse me, Miss? Is this seat taken?" A familiar voice broke through Ella's thoughts.

Ella looked straight up into those light hazel eyes, and her face lit up with joy. "Wyatt! Shouldn't you be sitting at some VIP table somewhere?"

Wyatt pulled out the chair next to Ella and sat down. "One of the great things about being the host – I get to sit wherever I want! And I want to sit next to you."

Ella blushed, smiling so wide she knew her cheeks would start to ache soon. As the dinner portion of the night continued, Ella and Wyatt talked non-stop as the different courses were placed in front of them. They both ate absentmindedly, occasionally commenting on the salmon or the potatoes, but were completely engrossed in their conversation. It was as if they were sitting alone at a restaurant, as opposed to in a giant ballroom surrounded by hundreds of people.

While Wyatt was in the middle of describing his nephew, Michael, Marissa once again interrupted them.

"There are a few members of the press here who are desperate to talk to you! They want to do a huge story. I'm talking photos of the party, photos of you, an interview with you and Charles—the whole thing. It's going to be unbelievable publicity!"

"Now?" Wyatt asked, a hint of annoyance in his voice.

"Well once you're finished with your dessert of course," Marissa tried for casual, but was unable to disguise the urgency.

Wyatt looked to Ella; his face unreadable.

"I understand!" Ella reassured him. "Go! It's for work." She smiled, hoping her disappointment wasn't showing.

"I'll only be a few minutes. Twenty minutes tops." He placed his hand over Ella's and gave it a gentle a squeeze. And then he was gone. Ella watched as he once again became swallowed up in the crowd.

The clock on her phone told her it was almost midnight, and she suddenly felt exhausted. The emotional highs and lows of the day were starting to catch up with her and she knew the night had to end soon. As she walked across the dance floor, she took in the scene one last time. Despite the feeling of disappointment creeping into her mind at the thought of having to wake up from this dream of a night, Ella couldn't help but smile at the group of people still in full celebration mode, dancing the night away. Alcohol and camaraderie had loosened up the once-stiff partygoers; bow ties and jackets had come off the men, and many women had kicked off their high heels and were dancing barefoot. Ella couldn't remember ever feeling that carefree. She always had to rush to a job or wake up early for a class. Right then and there, as she watched a pair of women pull up the hems of their expensive long gowns and tie them in knots so they no longer dragged on the floor, Ella made a decision that from this point forward she was going to make an effort to have a little fun.

During her first few years of college, Ella had befriended Kelly and Maya in her Intro to Early Education class. They would often invite her to go out for coffee after class or go out dancing on a Saturday night. Kelly and Maya would light up with excitement when they talked about Ice, a fancy club they sometimes went to, where celebrities hung out to enjoy bottle service and ear-pounding music. She had always politely turned down their offers, explaining that she had to work or study or have dinner at home with her mom. The truth was, clubs like Ice really weren't her scene. It wasn't long before the invitations stopped coming, and she found herself sitting alone in class, keeping her nose buried in her work, and leaving right after class to rush off to her next job. She never lingered in the student center to chat or joined a study group at the library. Her college experience was certainly different than most of her classmates, and that had never bothered her. Ella knew her path would be unique, and she never felt like she was missing out on anything. Until now.

The band slowed the music down and the drastic mood change snapped Ella out of her trance. As she continued to walk toward the elevators, she realized she still had Wyatt's tuxedo jacket draped over her shoulders. Scanning the crowd, she saw him standing at a high-top table, surrounded by a small crowd of eager-faced men and women reporters who were hurling questions at him, and hanging on his every word. One woman held her phone up toward Wyatt to record his responses, while a man with a big camera slung around his neck started snapping photos.

Ella wanted his gaze to meet hers one last time, but she resisted the urge to break up the interview and wrap her arms around his waist (imagine those photos in tomorrow's gossip section!). Instead she looked for Marissa, who was standing along the perimeter of the group surrounding Wyatt.

"Excuse me. It's Marissa, right?" Ella touched Marissa's arm to get her attention.

Marissa turned around and immediately flashed a smile at her. It must be an automatic response to anyone who came up to her.

"Yes, I'm Marissa," she answered, smiling even wider once she recognized who was standing before her.

Ella noted that Marissa was even more striking up close with her bright blue eyes, fair skin, and dark red lips. "I don't think we've officially met," Marissa held out her hand for Ella to shake.

She shook Marissa's hand firmly. "I'm Isabella, it's nice to meet you."

"Isabella, such a beautiful name. And who—?"

Before Marissa could continue, Ella interrupted her. "I have a favor to ask. Would you mind getting this back to Wyatt?" She held out the tuxedo jacket.

Eyeing her suspiciously, Marissa accepted the jacket, "Of course I will. But why? Are you on your way out?"

Ella nodded. "Yes, I need to leave. But please, thank Wyatt for me?" Without waiting for a reply, she gave Marissa one last smile before making her exit. Typically, not a crier, she was surprised by the flood of emotions rising within and threatening to spill over. For the entire elevator ride she kept her feelings in check, walking across the lobby with her head held high, still assuming the "Isabella" persona.

But as soon as she pushed through the outer lobby doors and walked into the cold December night, she could no longer hold it in. Tears streamed down her perfectly bronzed cheeks and smudged her expertly applied eye makeup. She hugged herself in the cold air, and then her heart stopped and panic set in—her coat. The beautiful white coat her mother had given her. She had left it at the coat check. What was she going to do? She couldn't go back up there, not now. She had barely escaped the first time without breaking down. What if she bumped into Wyatt, with her tear-stained face and mascara-ringed eyes? She wouldn't even know what to say to him. She had left, and even though she had said good-bye through Marissa, it was still a good-bye. Cinderella had left the ball before her gown turned into rags and there was no way to go back.

But still, indecision rooted her in place. She shivered in the cold; her bare arms now covered in goose bumps. Maybe she could call tomorrow and ask if she could come pick it up? With all that partying going on, she surely wouldn't be the only person to leave something behind. They'll have some type of lost and found pile, she assured herself. She would get the coat back, just not tonight.

Not right now. Right now, all she wanted to do was go home and climb into bed.

With that thought, Ella walked to the curb and held her hand up to hail a cab. At this time of night, cabs were aplenty, and one pulled up next to her in minutes. As she stepped into the cab, she thought she heard someone yell her name. She looked toward the double doors of the building and she saw him. Wyatt stood there, his face full of concern and confusion. She longed to run to him, to feel his strong arms around her, to breathe in his smell…but she knew it was over. She slammed the cab door shut and yelled, "Go!" at the driver. The driver, sensing how upset she was, and perhaps fearing she was in some type of danger, slammed on the gas and took off down Fifth Avenue. If Ella had looked back, which she wouldn't let herself do, she would have seen Wyatt racing to the curb, yelling after her.

Wyatt stood at the curb, hurt and disappointed. He watched the cab until its rear lights faded into the night. He walked back toward the building with his shoulders hunched and his head hanging down. As another car whizzed up the avenue, its headlights caught something shiny on the sidewalk. He reached down and picked up a necklace. It was a round gold pendant hanging from a delicate gold chain. On one side of the pendant were the words, *nunca dejes de soñar*, engraved in a pretty script. On the other side were the initials *IRM*. A little spark of hope ignited inside him. He would find her.

Chapter Ten

After a terrible night's sleep, Ella woke up on Monday morning with a pounding headache. The events of the night before swirled in her brain. The memory of Wyatt's body close to hers as they danced, his light hazel eyes serious and sincere. And the look on his face as he chased after her cab. And the coat! Her Abuela's coat! How was she going to get it back? Her mother would be devastated if she knew Ella had lost the nicest thing she had ever owned. The thought made Ella feel nauseated.

She dragged herself out of bed and trudged to the bathroom to take a shower. She was never more thankful her mother had to leave for work early in the morning, so she could have the apartment to herself for a little while. Also, she knew her mom would have a million questions about the party, and Ella was afraid if she spoke about the party, she would burst into tears.

In the shower she turned the water near-boiling hot, so it stung her skin, and she stood under it for a long time. She was forced to get out only when the hot water ran out and turned cold. She pulled her hair back into a ponytail, and its symbolism of returning to her normal life was not lost on her. The glamorous hair and makeup from the night before now felt more like a dream than reality. But the dream was over.

As she entered her tiny bedroom, she glanced at the clock on her nightstand. "Oh, no!" she yelled aloud. It was 9:45 a.m., and her first final exam was in Manhattan at ten. Her commute was usually close to forty-five minutes!

Cursing herself for being irresponsible and distracted, Ella threw on some yoga pants and a sweatshirt, grabbed her book bag, and sprinted out of the apartment and up the street to the train platform. She was now wide awake from all the adrenaline pumping through her veins, and she began to panic. If she missed this final, she might fail the class and therefore not graduate. All the time and money she spent that semester would be a total waste, and she would have to wait another whole semester to get her degree and begin applying for teaching jobs. The thought made her want to cry. This could not be happening. How could she let this happen?

After what felt like hours the train finally arrived. Sitting still and waiting as the train made all its stops on the way into Manhattan was pure torture. For the entire ride, Ella kept beating herself up mentally about her reckless behavior. *This* is what happened when she tried to have a night of carefree fun. Champagne and dancing—that was not her life. Her life was about focus and hard work, and as soon as she deviated from that course, *this* happened. She was about to lose something she had spent years working toward.

Ella was almost at the point of tears. She reached to her neck to grab hold of her gold pendant and channel her father but instead she was stricken with a whole new wave of panic. Nothing was there. Her hand frantically felt all around her neck, hysteria building with each passing second. *Maybe it's in my bed,* she thought, trying to calm herself down. Or maybe it fell off in the shower? Could it have gone down the drain? She tried to remember if she felt the necklace on her while in the shower and became almost certain she hadn't, which would mean she lost it while sleeping, or even worse—she could have lost it at the party.

On the verge of a breakdown, she closed her eyes and took deep calming breaths. The train stopped at the 14th Street station. Ella stood up and pulled herself together. *One thing at a time,* she told herself. First things first, she needed to get to that final. Pushing all thoughts of lost coats, lost necklaces, and those hazel eyes out of her mind, she raced to her school building. She wove in and out of the crowds on the sidewalk, yelling, "Sorry!" to anyone she bumped into. She entered the classroom around 10:30 a.m. —a half-hour late.

Frenzied and out of breath, she ran down the long aisle of seats, slowing down as she got closer to the professor's desk. The noise of her steps was the only sound in the hushed room. Most students were focused on the exam, undisturbed by Ella's disruption. No one even looked up as Ella made her way toward the front of the room. She took a few deep breaths and tried to calm down as she approached Professor Maltin.

Professor Maltin was reading some papers as she approached him. She cleared her throat to get his attention. Without moving his head, he raised his eyes, his glasses perched on the end of his nose, and glanced up at Ella.

"I'm really sorry I'm late. I had a crazy morning…" Ella began, her mind spinning to come up with a decent excuse. She was pretty sure the truth wasn't going to cut it. "Could I please still sit for the final, now?"

Her heart pounded in her chest as she awaited Professor Maltin's reply.

"Ms. Martinez, is it? He asked her, now sitting straight up and taking off his glasses. Ella nodded. "Ms. Martinez, this is very unlike you. You have had perfect attendance all year long, am I right?"

"Yes, sir."

"Since this is out of character for you, and you have worked diligently all year long, I'm going to let you take the exam. However, you only have the original allotted time. Which means everyone else had from ten to eleven o'clock, and you will also only have until eleven o'clock." Ella let this news sink in, partly relieved that she would be able to take the exam, and partly panicked at only having less than half the time the rest of the class had to take it.

Professor Maltin handed her the test. "I suggest you get started."

"Yes, sir. Thank you, sir." Ella grabbed the test and rushed to the first open seat to begin.

The familiar chime of the door at The Book Nook did nothing to calm Ella's nerves. After the insane morning she had, she felt a mixture of frazzled, heartbroken, desperate, and exhausted. Marney took one look at her and knew something was up. "Oh no, what's wrong, my Isabella? What happened? Is it your mom?"

Ella shook her head, barely holding in the tears. "No, but if she knew everything that happened today, she would probably have a heart attack."

"Oh dear, come here. Come tell me everything," Marney motioned with her hand for Ella to sit by her. "Let me get you some tea. You take your coat off and relax. I'm sure once you've talked about it, you'll realize it's not as bad as you think."

Ella did as she was told, taking off her coat and sitting down in the comfy chair in the corner. Marney, her emerald green and purple caftan making her appear to float as she moved, brought over a giant mug of steaming tea. "Okay, now start from the beginning. How was the party?" Marney's eyes danced with anticipation.

Thinking of the party, Ella couldn't help but smile. "The party was unbelievable. Magical, even." Ella filled Marney in on everything, from the décor to the music and the gifts and, of course, Wyatt.

Marney clasped her hands together at her chest, bouncing with joy. "I *knew* it, I *just knew* it!" she declared.

"Before you get too excited, let me finish," Ella warned. She then explained how she left without saying good-bye, and how she couldn't sleep last night, which brought her to the disastrous morning.

"Oh my, well *that is* bad." Marney's eyes squinted with concern.

"Thanks, Marney. Really helpful," Ella moaned, rolling her eyes.

"I'm sorry. Let's tackle one problem at a time. First, have you tried calling someone to ask about the coat?"

Ella shook her head. "No, I haven't had a chance to. And who should I call? The main lobby of the building? The law office?"

"I think you should call that Marissa lady. She seemed to be the one in charge of everything."

"*I cannot* call her. They can't know who I am! I wasn't even supposed to be there last night. I broke all the rules and now I'm paying for it."

"You don't have to give her your name. Better yet, make up a fake name. If she has the coat, we'll deal with it. Maybe you can ask her to leave it in the lobby for you?"

Ella nodded, feeling a little better. "That might work."

"And now the next problem—your exam." Ella groaned, thinking of the exam. "What is the worst grade you can get and still pass the class?" Marney asked.

"I don't want to just pass the class; I want to do well!"

"After today, that ship might have sailed."

Ella dropped her head into her hands, hiding her face. "Ugh! I had an A in the class going into finals. But the final is half our grade."

"I'm no mathematician but I think you could probably get a D on the exam and still pass the class, right?"

"I guess so," Ella moaned at the thought of getting a C in a class that she had worked hard to maintain an A average in.

"Do you think you at least got a D on the exam?" Marney asked her.

"I only finished a little more than half of it, but the questions I did finish, I'm pretty sure I got most of them correct."

Marney jumped up and clapped her hands together. "See there? Nothing to worry about, Ella! You know all the information you need to know to move on and become an excellent teacher, and that's all that matters. You will pass your class and graduate!"

Ella had never thought about college that way. All she really had to do was get a good enough grade to pass the class and get her degree. She took a deep breath and sank back in the chair as a sense of relief washed over her. And then she remembered her necklace, and she got all stressed out again. Out of habit, Ella put her hand up to her throat and felt the emptiness where her precious pendant once hung.

Marney watched Ella blindly searching for a necklace that wasn't there and was just as worried as Ella about it being gone. The necklace could be anywhere—in the cab, in her bed, down the drain. It was like trying to find a needle in a haystack—or a necklace in the jungle of New York City. "Don't you worry about the necklace," Marney said firmly, her faux confidence defying her concern. "Things have a way of working out. I know that necklace will find its way back to you." She gently squeezed Ella's arm.

Forcing a smile, Ella nodded her head. The door chimed and Marney left to tend to the customer. She sat still, unable to push the vision of Wyatt's smile out of her mind. Aside from the coat, the necklace, and her finals there was Wyatt and the crushing feeling she may never see him again.

"Alright, missy," Marney came over to Ella and shook her finger at her. "That's enough sulking for one day. It's time to get that coat back. And I know exactly how to do it!"

Following Marney's command, Ella followed her to the back office. "What did you say that woman's name was? Melissa? The one that works at the law firm?"

"Marissa," Ella corrected her. "Why?"

"I'm going to call her, that's why," Marney said as she hunched over her old desktop computer, her face only inches from the screen as she squinted to read the website.

Ella paused before responding, trying to decide if this was a genius idea, or if this was going to be a total disaster. She had a feeling the latter might be the case. But what choice did she have? Her mother would be crushed if she knew she had lost the only nice piece of clothing she had ever owned. She must get that coat back, no matter what the consequences. Except if the consequences were Wyatt, by way of Marissa, finding out Ella's identity and how she came to be at that party. Marney was her only hope. Oh. No.

"Is that her? Right there—the pretty blonde?" Marney was pointing to a photo on the computer screen. Ella leaned over her shoulder and saw she had pulled up Marissa's bio on the company website. As they read Marissa's long list of accomplishments, including lots of summa cum laude this and Ivy League that, Ella felt even more inadequate. She sighed.

"What is it, dear? Is this not her?" Marney turned around to face her.

"That is definitely her." She kept staring at Marissa's photo.

"Well okay then, let's rock n' roll," Marney said, nodding her head as she picked up the Book Nook's telephone.

"Wait, should you be using the store's phone? What if Marissa tracks you down here?" Ella knew she sounded paranoid, but she couldn't help herself.

"Haven't you ever heard of star six seven?" Marney's eyes filled with mischief.

"What the heck is star six seven?" she asked.

"The cell phone generation," Marney sighed as shook her head. "Such a shame you never learned some of the most useful tactics to use when you don't want to be discovered. You know, like when you want to call a boy and see if he's home, but you don't want him to know it's you checking in on him? You press star six seven before you dial the number! And the person you're calling can't see the number calling them. Watch this!"

Marney could barely contain her excitement as she punched the numbers into the old landline telephone.

"Hello, could you put me through to Marissa Mulvaney's office please." Her voice took on an unfamiliar formal tone. Ella was impressed. "This is Regina Smith."

Hearing her mother's first name used, Ella tapped Marney on the shoulder and silently mouthed "No!" She gestured her arms wildly. "Why?" she whispered, her eyes bugging out of her head. Marney calmly shrugged, and looked at Ella like, "What? Did I do something wrong?"

With an eye roll to show more of her displeasure, she tuned back in to Marney's phone conversation.

"Yes, hello Marissa, how are you? My name is Regina White and I am Tinsley Golden's personal assistant. Tinsley was the date of one of your young associates last night, and she left her coat at the party by mistake. I would like to swing by the building today and pick it up for her."

Marney paused as she listened to whatever it was Marissa was saying. "Who was Tinsley's date?" She looked to Ella to come up with a name, and Ella shook her head back and forth.

"Umm, she was Michael's date," Marney said matter-of-factly, and quickly continued, "The coat is white cashmere with a fur collar, and it is very important to Miss Golden. I would like to come pick it up today. I'm sure you had a lost and found from the event?" Marney paused once again to listen. The suspense was killing Ella. If only she could hear what Marissa was saying!

"Yes, thank you. No, I will call you back in about an hour. Will that give you enough time to look?" Pause. "Great. Until then. Bye now."

"That was torture! Oh, my goodness, Marney! Tinsley Golden?" Ella couldn't help herself and started giggling. "Where on earth did you come up with that name?" She was now full-blown laughing, tears running down her cheeks.

Marney gestured toward Merry, her golden retriever who was, as usual, sprawled out in the corner taking one of her many dog naps. And they both burst into a joint fit of laughter.

"You really are one of a kind," Ella managed to get out after finally catching her breath. "But wait, why do you have to call her back?"

"She is going to look for the coat and said she would call me back. Obviously, I didn't want that, so I said I would call her back."

"Let's hope she doesn't ask any more questions about Michael. Why did you use that name, anyway?"

"I figured almost every office has a Michael, and maybe if we're lucky, more than one."

Ella nodded in agreement.

"Now we have to wait an hour. Ugh. What should we do while we wait?"

"Do you have an exam to study for?" Marney raised an eyebrow.

Ella's shoulders sagged. Normally she would use slow days, like Monday mornings, as time for schoolwork. Marney was right, she still had four more final exams this week. She had an hour to kill and she should be using her time wisely. But how in the world was she going to concentrate on her exams right now?

Begrudgingly picking up her school bag, Ella trudged toward the back room. "This is why I should never have gone to that party," she muttered.

"What was that, honey?" Marney asked. "I thought we decided the pity party was over."

Ella spun back around to face Marney. "I've spent the last six years of my life, working, working, working. I kept my head down and I did the right thing. I sacrificed a lot," Ella's voice cracked. "And for what? One silly night out? I got distracted and tried to be somebody I'm not. That's not me and that's not my life. And now I'm about to lose everything that's important to me."

As she walked toward the back room, hunched over and upset, Marney wracked her brain to find some comforting words, but none came. She wanted to explain to Ella that it's these times— the times of heartache, disappointment, confusion, and worry— these were the times that mattered the most. This was proof of life! Ella had been so focused on her goal of getting a degree without taking out any loans, she ended up completely isolating herself. She was right about one thing; she had sacrificed a lot.

Last night, as Ella strutted out of The Book Nook in that gorgeous gown, her spirit had come alive. Marney wasn't going to let her forget what it felt like to see the world in a whole new way. She had to figure out a way to help and she was pretty sure it started with finding that coat.

The store was quiet and literally all Marney could hear was the ticking of the clock. An antique grandfather clock sat against the front wall of the store, and she found herself watching the pendulum swing back and forth to mark the seconds as they passed. She wandered around straightening bookshelves and re-shelving children's books that had been scattered around the kids' corner the night before. The front bell chimed, and she rushed to welcome the customer, acting overly attentive. She welcomed every distraction—anything to help pass the time.

Finally, Marney saw the little hand had crept all the way around the face of the clock; an hour had passed since she had called Marissa. It was time to make the follow-up call. As she made her way to the back room, Ella was coming out toward her. The two women looked at each other knowingly, and Marney gave a slight nod.

"It's time." Ella's eyes were wide and her face somber. You would have thought they were about to speak with a doctor about a dire medical diagnosis, not learn the location of a coat.

Marney dialed the phone, once again using the old-school star-six-seven before entering the numbers to Marissa's office. After going through the same song and dance with the secretary, all the Tinsley Golden and Regina White silliness, she was patched through to Marissa.

Ella squeezed her eyes shut and held her breath as she listened to Marney's side of the conversation, trying to decipher if the news was good or bad, but Marney was giving her nothing. Her tone stayed constant and even. It was driving Ella crazy.

"Okay, great. I appreciate all your help. Yes. Okay. That will work. Bye now."

Ella opened her eyes, looking to Marney for some type of clue. Was she going to get her coat back or was she going to have to go home and break her mother's heart?

"So?" She kept looking at Marney expectantly, keeping her panic in check.

"I'm going to pick it up later today," Marney smiled at Ella.

"They have it! Oh my. Thank god!" Ella jumped up with her hands together as if she were praying. "Oh Marney, how can I ever thank you enough!" Ella lunged at her friend and wrapped her arms around her. Marney laughed. "Don't be silly—it's nothing, really! And hold off on all the thank yous until we have it in our hands. We still have a bit of planning to do."

A few hours later, after a quick call to Nancy Jenkins, the only other employee of The Book Nook; Ella and Marney were on their way to 430 Fifth Avenue.

"What's the plan?" Ella asked Marney as they sat in the back of a yellow cab.

"The coat is being left with reception at Dawson & Hancock," Marney explained. "We shouldn't have to have any contact with Marissa. I'm going to walk in, get the coat, and walk out. Easy-peasy."

"What if Marissa happens to see you?"

"That won't matter. She doesn't even know my real name!"

"What if they ask you for your driver's license to prove you are who you say you are? Which you aren't!" Ella couldn't explain it, but although this little excursion to pick up the coat seemed simple, she had a nagging feeling that it wasn't going to be "easy-peasy."

"I'll figure something out," Marney smiled at Ella and reached for her hand. "Don't look so worried! I'm an old lady, no one's going to give me a hard time!"

Sweat started to form on Ella's brow the second they entered the lobby of 430 Fifth Avenue. Her eyes quickly darted to the security desk to see who was working. Thankfully it wasn't anyone she recognized. She knew the night security, not the daytime crew. At least that was one less thing to worry about.

"What do you plan to do, dear?" Marney calmly asked Ella as they stood next to one of the giant faux Christmas trees in the lobby, pretending to admire the generic red and gold ball ornaments.

"I don't know. Should I stay down here? Or should I go up with you and wait by the elevators on the 22nd floor? What do you think?" Ella's eyes were darting all over the place and her speech was rushed.

"I think you should stay down here," Marney said, smiling. "I'll be back in a jiffy!" Without waiting for Ella to reply, she turned on her heels and glided across the lobby, as only she could. Even her resting face held a smile, and she always looked like she didn't have a care in the world. She was a little too relaxed, in Ella's mind.

Ella held her breath as she watched Marney approach the security desk and speak with the female security officer on duty. The two seemed to be chatting an awful long time, and her heart began to pound. What if they don't let her up the elevator? What if they ask for her license?

A loud familiar laugh echoed through the lobby. Ella watched as Marney threw her head back and shared another hearty laugh with everyone within a fifty-yard radius. The security guard, a broad shouldered, six-foot tall, intimidating blonde was laughing along with her, as if the two were old friends. Ella shook her head from side to side. Only Marney. A minute later the guard handed Marney a guest pass and led her to the elevator bank.

Breathing a sigh of relief, Ella finally relaxed for the first time all day. She walked over to the set of large windows overlooking Fifth Avenue. There were a few newspaper racks in front of the windows, and she started glancing at the headlines of all the different papers. From the corner of her eye she saw someone walking toward the swinging doors which were right next to her. She turned to look at the person and her breath became stuck in her throat. Wyatt Dawson was striding across the lobby and heading straight toward the doors.

She spun around and grabbed a *New York Post*, quickly placing it in front of her face. Very slowly, she pulled down a corner of the paper so she could sneak glances of him, soaking in every inch of his beautiful face, trying to etch it into her memory. His brow was furrowed and his expression serious, as if he had a lot on his mind. He walked briskly and with a sense of purpose. People seemed to be able to sense he was coming and moved out of the way for him to pass.

Once he was through the swinging doors and out on the sidewalk, Ella let herself stare openly. There was very little chance he would recognize her the way she looked today, she reasoned. Her hair was pulled back into a tight bun and the only makeup she wore was mascara. Her all-black ensemble blended in with the New

York City masses. He wouldn't have looked twice at her if she walked straight into him. Her heart pounded in her chest and her stomach was a swirl of nerves. She was grateful he hadn't seen her, and disappointed at the same time. She wanted his eyes on her one more time, to feel his hand on her lower back, to smell his musky cologne. She needed to sit down. The lobby had no seats (they probably didn't want people loitering, she guessed), so she sat on the ledge of the window. Her legs felt wobbly and weak. She still had some time to kill before Marney got back and she needed a distraction, she opened the newspaper that was clenched in her hands. She read a few pages and then turned to read the gossip on Page Six. Much to her surprise, she saw her own face staring back at her.

Right there at the top of the page was a giant photo of Ella and Wyatt dancing together at the Christmas party. Her face was unknowingly turned toward the camera and she was smiling as Wyatt appeared to be whispering something in her ear. Below the photo the caption read:

> *Hearts are breaking all over Manhattan today.*
> *Wyatt Dawson, New York City's Most Eligible Bachelor, may not be a bachelor any longer. But who is the beautiful woman who has stolen his heart? The Post wants to know. Do you know the identity of this mystery woman? Email us and give us the scoop!*

Ella read the blurb repeatedly. Each time her eyes swept over the words, "beautiful woman who has stolen his heart", her pulse ticked up a notch. Had she really stolen his heart? Was he thinking about her as much as she was thinking about him? It couldn't be. This was Wyatt Dawson! He had women willing to cheat and steal to get an invitation to a Christmas party he was hosting. He couldn't possibly still be wondering about Ella…or could he?

Ella stared at the woman in the photo, and the woman looked like a stranger. But then something deep down in her soul stirred. It was an emotion she couldn't quite pinpoint. Could it be pride? A small smile spread across her face. She closed her eyes and was taken back to that moment on the rooftop deck — he leaned in to speak to her, the warmth of his body next to hers, his strong arms wrapped around her, his whisper tickling her ear…

"Excuse me, Miss. Miss?"

Ella opened her eyes to see a member of the building security team. He was average height, with pockmarked skin and his hair was cropped almost to the scalp. His heavy eyelids hung down over his eyes, making him appear either bored or tired, or perhaps both.

"Can I help you?" she asked as politely as she could muster, having been pulled out of a beautiful daydream.

"Miss, I'm going to have to ask you not to sit on the ledge of the window, please."

And just like that, she was back to reality.

Chapter Eleven

The reception area of the offices of Dawson & Hancock was modern, and a tad too masculine for Marney's taste. The neutrals upon neutrals, with straight lines and layered textures was a style she would never get used to. Where was the color, for heaven's sake? With her emerald green and purple blouse, Marney's outfit provided the only color in the room, and she liked that. After giving her name and the reason for her visit to the young, chic woman behind the front desk, she took a seat on an uncomfortable sofa. Her bracelets jangled as she picked up a magazine from the side table. It was an *Architectural Digest*, not really her thing, but she'd give it a shot.

Much to her surprise she found herself enjoying an article about an Italian seaside palace. The photos were dreamy, and she felt herself swept away to a time many years ago when she was traveling through Europe, full of energy and ambition. She couldn't help but let out a sigh filled nostalgia, not sadness. She was quite content with how she lived her life and the choices she made.

"Ms. White? Ms. Regina White?" Marney broke free from her Italian daydream, remembering her stage name perhaps a few seconds too late. One good thing about being old was that people assumed your hearing was going. She got away with a lot, thanks to people's assumptions about the elderly, and she was okay with that.

Marney cleared her throat and stood up to address the woman who had walked into the reception area and called her name. The woman was in her mid-forties, she guessed. Her classic navy skirt, matching boxy suit jacket, and short no-nonsense haircut spoke volumes about her personality. Meaning, she didn't have much of a personality.

"Hello, yes, I'm Ms. White," Marney gave the woman a small, polite smile, not the wide, warm version she would normally offer to people she was meeting. She wanted to appear professional.

"You're Ms. White? The personal assistant to…" the woman looked down at some sort of tablet. "…to a Ms. Tinsley Golden?"

The made-up name being spoken aloud by this very serious woman (attorney? executive assistant? Marney wasn't sure) almost made her laugh as she suddenly found the whole situation quite humorous. But for Ella's sake, she had to see this through, which meant she had to play the part.

"That is correct," Marney said, nodding her head for emphasis. The other woman's skepticism was abundantly clear. "Why, am I not what you were expecting?"

The woman's eyes widened, but the rest of her face gave nothing away. She stood up straighter. "It's, well, typically…" The woman squirmed under Marney's glare.

"What? I'm a lot older than most assistants? Is that what you're trying to say?" Marney squinted her eyes, trying to look angry. "Ha! If I had a dollar for every time I have been met with this type of age discrimination, I'd be a millionaire, I tell you!" Her voice had gotten incrementally louder as her soliloquy continued. She was having quite a bit of fun, truth be told. "What, you reach a certain age and you're supposed to go into hiding until you die? Is that what our society wishes to do with its aging population? Well guess what, sweetheart? *You* will be old one day too! That's right, I know it's hard to imagine now…but you will!" Marney pointed a finger at her, slightly aggressively.

"No, no, no," the woman said quickly, shaking her head from side to side. She was in full panic mode at this point, trying to find a way to remove the foot that she had lodged in her mouth. "I apologize, ma'am, miss, Ms. White, that is not what I meant at all. It came out completely wrong. Never mind what I was trying to say, it doesn't matter. It was nothing. Are you okay?"

Marney had been pacing the small waiting area during her monologue, which, incidentally, she totally nailed! And now, with her hands on her hips she stopped, took a dramatic deep breath, and nodded her head, signaling she was ready to move on.

"Okay," the woman said, visibly relieved. "You are here to collect a certain coat that was left behind at the Christmas party last night, is that correct?"

"That is correct. And honestly, I'm still a bit upset. If it's okay with you, I would like to take the coat and be on my way." This was certainly the way to avoid too many questions.

Anxious to be rid of her, the navy suit woman started nodding her head rapidly. "Of course, I completely understand." She walked behind the receptionist's desk, who was doing her best to pretend she hadn't witnessed the whole dramatic exchange and picked up a large shopping bag.

Marney held out her hand without saying a word, and the woman handed her the bag. With a quick glance in the bag to be sure it was indeed Ella's coat; she gave the woman a curt nod and marched toward the door with a satisfied smile on her face.

The woman in the navy suit and the receptionist shared a relieved look once Marney walked out the door. Meanwhile, Marney all but danced her way to the elevator bank. Maybe she should have been an actress, because *that* was an Academy-winning performance right there!

Marney was still beaming with satisfaction when the elevator doors opened. Much to her surprise, a pretty blonde in a perfectly tailored black sheath dress stepped out into the lobby. Marissa Mulvaney. Marney was hoping her age would help her out here, too—most young people look right past older people as if they weren't even there. She hadn't thought to bring her large hessonite garnet gemstone, which was supposed to bring good luck, she crossed her fingers and tried for a generic smile as she waited politely for Marissa to exit the elevator.

Whether it was simply her nerves, or the universe's plan, she would never know, but as Marissa walked by, the big shopping bag holding *the* coat hit her ever so lightly on the leg. However, it was surprising enough for Marissa to pause and look straight at Marney, down at the bag, and back at Marney again.

"Oh, you're the woman I spoke to earlier. Someone-Golden's assistant, is it?"

Marney nodded quickly and smiled, holding her hand in front of the elevator doors so they wouldn't close before she had a chance to slip in. "Yes, that's me! And you are Ms. Mulvaney?"

Marissa nodded and her perfectly made-up face broke into a smile. "It's very nice to meet you, Ms. White. Is that the coat in the bag?"

"It is, thank you for finding if for my—for Miss Golden. She will be quite relieved."

"I'm happy to help. Did she have fun at the party?"

Marney smiled a real smile. "She said she had a magnificent time! She looked gorgeous in that red dress and she said the music and the food were spectacular."

After all the work Marissa had put into it, she loved hearing how much people appreciated it. "I am so glad! And a red dress, hmmm? who did you say Ms. Golden's date was?"

"Oh, did I say red dress? I don't know what I was thinking. She was wearing a black dress, or was it blue? You know, I'm not quite sure what she was wearing, come to think of it. Me with my old eyes and all."

Marissa cocked her head to the side to study Marney a little closer. Some of her co-workers would joke with her, calling her the human lie detector. Whether that was from years of working in human resources, or innate gut instinct, she didn't know. But what she did know? This little old lady with the waves of gray hair, bright clothes and layers of jewelry was lying to her. But why? Before she could ask her again about this Tinsley Golden person's date, the older woman spoke first.

"Thank you again for finding Miss Golden's jacket. I do have one other question, if you don't mind?"

Startled that the woman wanted to keep this conversation going when only a second ago she looked like she was ready to run down the twenty-two flights of stairs to get away from her, Marissa nodded for her to continue. Regina White had piqued her curiosity.

"Of course, what can I help you with?"

"You didn't happen to find a gold necklace, did you? When you were cleaning up after the party?"

"No, not that I know of. Why? Did your employer lose her necklace as well?"

"I'm afraid she did." Marney pushed on the elevator door again which had been trying to close for the last few minutes. "Okay, then, I'll be on my way! Cheerio!" She quickly slipped into the elevator and smiled as the doors closed, leaving a confused and suspicious Marissa on the other side.

Banished from her seat on the window ledge, Ella spent what felt like an eternity pacing the lobby floor as she waited for Marney. The security guards glanced her way every few minutes, but she ignored them. She didn't care if they thought she was crazy. Her mind was spinning, and she needed to keep her body moving in order to give all the energy someplace to go. This morning her heart was filled with despair at the thought of never seeing Wyatt again, and now she had almost come face-to-face with him! And the newspaper article! That article solidified that last night hadn't been a dream. It had been real. The connection she'd felt was real. And people had noticed, or at least one person had—whoever it was that took the picture of them. Who would have taken their photo? A jealous woman?

Ella felt a tap on her back and she slowly turned around, fearing it would be Wyatt. It was Marney. Disappointment made her shoulders droop a little. Why would it be Wyatt?

"Marney!" She wrapped her arms around her sweet friend. "How did it go? Did you get the coat? Did you see Marissa? Or Wyatt? Oh wait, you couldn't have seen Wyatt, I watched him leave."

Marney smiled a knowing smile. "Ohhh, now I understand why you're flapping around like a flamingo. You saw Wyatt!" Marney clapped her hands together.

"Do flamingos flap around?"

Marney shrugged off the comment. "Now that you and Mr. Dawson have met, the universe is going to keep throwing you two together. Mark my words, this is not the last you'll see of him," she said sternly, shaking her finger at her.

Ella rolled her eyes. "Did you get the coat?"

Marney lifted the shopping bag and showed Ella the contents. "That's it, right?"

Ella reached into the bag and felt the soft fabric, exhaling with relief. She had her coat back. "Marney, I cannot thank you enough for this!" Ella hugged her so hard Marney was afraid she might break a bone. "What would I do without you?" Ella pulled back and looked at Marney, the threat of tears choking her up.

"Oh, don't be silly," Marney said, waving her off. "It is nice to see you smile again, but I'm afraid it's not all good news."

Ella looked at her quizzically.

"I happened to run into Marissa Mulvaney on the way out of the office. I asked her if anyone had found a gold necklace after the party, and I'm afraid not. No necklace was found."

"Wait, you talked to Marissa? Did she ask you a bunch of questions? Tell me exactly what was said." Any sense of relief was now quickly replaced by mild panic. Again.

"Don't be such a worrywart, Ella! I handled it like a pro, trust me. It was quite a performance, if I do say so myself. When she mentioned the red dress, I totally threw her off. By the end, she didn't know which way was up," Marney giggled.

"Now she knows I wore a red dress and lost a necklace? This isn't good, Marney." Ella shook her head. "What if she puts it all together? And then she tells Wyatt? I don't know what I'll do!"

Placing her hands on Ella's shoulders, Marney spoke softly. "Ella, honey, there is no possible way Marissa, or Wyatt for that matter, could find out who you are. They have no name! You aren't on the guest list! Please don't worry."

Ella nodded. Her friend was right, of course. There was no way they could figure out who she was.

"But, if they did somehow find out, what is the worst that could happen? Would it really be terrible if Wyatt knew who you were?"

"It would be awful. The woman he met that night, Isabella, is not who I am. I want him to remember her."

"Isabella *is* Ella! You are one and the same! He was interested in *you*, and what you have in here." She pointed to Ella's heart. "I wish you would be proud of who you are and what you have to offer."

Ella saw a man in a suit walking toward them. Alarmed, she grabbed Marney by the arm and rushed them out the swinging doors of the building.

"What? What's wrong?" Marney asked.

She whipped back around and watched the man walk out the doors and onto the sidewalk. Of course, it wasn't Wyatt. He had already left. She was officially losing her mind. She looked at Marney's worried expression and felt terrible. "I'm sorry, Marney. I was afraid…I thought…"

"You thought you saw Wyatt walking toward us, so you rushed out into the cold to avoid him?"

Ella looked down at her hands. Shame crept up her neck and turned her face red.

"Okay, let's get back to The Book Nook. Hopefully Nancy isn't totally overwhelmed working alone." Marney put her arm around Ella's waist as they turned to walk uptown. When Marney saw her friend's response to the strange man in the lobby, she was even more worried about her than she dared admit. She had to find a way to fix this; of that she was certain.

Chapter Twelve

How could he have not gotten her last name? He could see forgetting to ask for her phone number, since they were so caught up in the night's activities, but how did he not even ask her last name? These thoughts, and many more just like them, swam around in Wyatt's mind the whole night after the party, and now the entire next day.

Another thought that also squeezed its way in and played on his self-doubt— Isabella knew who he was, she knew his name and where he worked, yet she hadn't tried to contact him. Had he done something wrong? Is that why she left without saying good-bye? Was she annoyed by all the time he'd had to spend talking to the press? Well, if that were true, then maybe it would be better if he never saw her again. His job never turned off, and if that bothered her, then she wasn't right for him anyway.

Although that sounded logical and was a good attempt at rationalizing the whole thing, it didn't quite work. After speaking with Isabella for those few hours at the party, he couldn't see her as someone who would get angry at him for having a business responsibility. It didn't fit with what little he knew of her.

Leaning back in his desk chair, he stopped staring at his computer and looked out the window at the city sprawled out before him. It's not like he was getting any work done anyway. The *Post* was perched on his desk. He flicked it open as a welcome distraction.

Or maybe not so welcome. Staring back at him was a photo of him and Isabella dancing, their bodies close to one another. He quickly scanned the blurb, his heart thumping in his chest as he read. Who had taken this photo and sent it to the paper? Even in the grainy picture, Isabella looked like a Christmas angel. Had he really been so lucky to be that close to her, his hand on her back, whispering in her ear? Until seeing the photo, he had been wondering if the feelings and chemistry between them had been a figment of his imagination. But this photo was proof—proof that the relaxed, easy dynamic between them was real. By the end of the night, it felt as if they had known each other for years.

He leaned back once again, placing the paper back on his desk. His eyes caught a glimpse of something shiny lying next to the paper. The necklace. He suddenly knew what had to be done.

"Alice! Send Marissa Mulvaney to see me asap, please," Wyatt barked into his phone to his assistant.

He might not know Isabella's last name, but he knew two things: He was going to get to the bottom of whoever was sending photos of him to the press; and he was going to find Isabella.

With renewed enthusiasm, Wyatt grabbed a legal pad and started to make a list. What did he learn from his conversation with Isabella last night that would be useful in finding her? He wrote a few things down:

1. *Works at a bookstore*
2. *Volunteers at a community center*
3. *Is half Puerto Rican and half Italian*
4. *Lives in New York City (which borough?)*

As he stared at the list, he realized it was short and vague. He picked up the gold necklace and saw the initials on the back of the pendant—*ILM.* He added one more item to his list:

5. *Her last name begins with an M*

There was a knock on his office door, and without taking his eyes off his list, Wyatt called out, "Come in!"

101

"Mr. Dawson, hello. Alice said you'd like to see me?"

"Yes," Wyatt looked up at Marissa who was standing in front of his desk. "I need your help with a special assignment."

"Of course, anything you need. Now that the Christmas party is over, I have a lot more time. Do you need some help with your Christmas shopping? I still have a list of what we sent your nieces and nephews last year, I can check to be sure we don't send any repeats this year."

"No, that's not it." Wyatt looked back at his list. "But now that you mention it, I was thinking *I* would shop for them this year. You know, by myself."

Marissa's eyebrows went up in surprise, "Wow, that's really great of you. If it's not Christmas shopping, what is it you want me to help you with?"

"I need you to track down someone that was at the party last night."

"Sure, I have a list of everyone who was there. Who are you looking for?"

Wyatt's face lit up. "Really? You know the names of everyone who was at the party last night?"

"Of course," Marissa smiled, "Well, almost everyone. Why? Is it a member of the press you're looking for?"

"Yes, that too. Who was there from the *Post*?"

"There were a few people there from the *Post*, I can email you their names and contact information."

"That would be great. I have to say, I am not thrilled with the photos of me that have been in the paper lately. New York City's Most Eligible Bachelor? I mean, come on. That's not how we want the public viewing me, is it? How is anyone going to take me seriously with that silly title being attached to my name? As the head of public relations at this firm, I expect you to handle this. I don't want to see any more photos of me in any newspaper, and not one more mention of this Most Eligible Bachelor thing."

Marissa stayed uncharacteristically quiet.

"What, you don't agree with me?" he asked her. "You should see the emails I'm getting from random women all over the city. It's ridiculous. And it's a waste of my time."

"I...I think it's a good thing for people to see the more human, more relatable side of you."

"I haven't appeared human in the past?"

"Not exactly; you haven't been relatable. Image is very important when a potential client is considering using our firm. We want them to feel welcomed—like they're coming home," Marissa smiled warmly.

Wyatt rolled his eyes. "I think most people want to know if I can win their case. And guess what? I can. That's why people come to us. Not because I'm an eligible bachelor."

Marissa opened her mouth to speak again, and he held up his hand, palm out, to stop her. "I'm not going to change my mind on this, Marissa. Fix it. Please."

She nodded once, and wanting to change the subject she asked, "What was the other thing you wanted to ask me? Did you want me to find the contact information of someone at the party?"

"Yes, right." Wyatt took a deep breath. "There was a woman at the party, she was wearing a red dress and her name was Isabella, but that's all I know about her. I want to find out who she is. You can do that, right? Maybe find out who she came with?"

Marissa took all this information in, showing no outward reaction to the request. "Yes, of course. I can find her."

"Great," Wyatt said, smiling with satisfaction. "If you could do that today, I would appreciate it."

With another quick nod, she left Wyatt's office. On her way back to her own office, she tried to decide if she was more shocked by the fact that he was doing his own Christmas shopping this year, or that he asked her to track down a woman. His discontent with the articles in the paper, well, that she expected. However, when his anger subsided a little, she would be sure to point out that he was staring at the photo of the woman in red when she walked into his office. She was pretty sure that photo was the spark that ignited his desire to find her. Who was this mysterious woman? Now Marissa was determined to find out, too.

As soon as Marissa left his office, Wyatt turned back toward his computer. He opened a browser and did a search for "independent bookstores nyc." There were pages that listed "The Top 30 Bookstores in NYC" with a map of the city marking the different locations of stores with red pins. The problem, he quickly realized, was that he didn't know if the bookstore she worked at was in Manhattan. She might work in one of the other boroughs. Not for the first time today, he wished he'd had more time with her. He wished he'd been able to ask her more questions. Starting with, "What is your last name?"

Focusing on determination, not frustration, he started a list. He wrote down all thirty bookstores mentioned in that one article, and then picked up the phone and started calling them one by one. If he treated this like he was doing research for one of his client's cases, he knew he would prevail.

He dialed the number for the first bookstore he had written down, one called "Books Are Magic." As soon as he heard the phone ring, he realized he wasn't sure what he would say. *Is there a beautiful woman named Isabella that works there? She is in her early to mid-twenties and her last name begins with an M?* That sounded good. He would give that a try.

He called a few places, with no luck, before Alice knocked on his door with some pressing work for one of his cases. Oh yeah, work. He needed to do that. She also reminded him that he had a meeting in the Hudson Yards neighborhood. He should be leaving for that soon, too. He took one last look at his list, sighed, and vowed to get back to it later. Maybe by then Marissa would have some information on the mysterious Isabella and he wouldn't have to continue with this process, anyway. He grabbed his overcoat and headed to the elevator bank.

The rest of Wyatt's day passed by in a flash. Work kept him busy and his mind occupied, but every now and then, when he was in a cab or walking from one meeting to another, he would let his mind wander. And it wandered right back to Isabella. He tried to picture what she would be doing right now. Could she be in class, or at the bookstore or the community center? Was she thinking about him?

After a client dinner at Quality Meats, a steakhouse in Midtown, he was exhausted. He hadn't slept well after the party last night, and now this long dinner had done him in. He didn't have any energy left to go back to the office, and the only reason he wanted to go back was to work on finding Isabella. Bookstores were closed at that time of night anyway, so it wasn't as if he could continue making calls. He checked his email from his phone on the cab ride uptown to his apartment and after quickly scanning through them all he was disappointed when he didn't see one from Marissa. Had she not found Isabella either? First thing in the morning, he would call her into his office and ask for an update.

Wyatt stared out the window for the remainder of the cab ride up to Central Park West. Normally he would have used this time to respond to the inbox full of unopened emails, but tonight he wasn't in the mood. Instead of keeping his head down to stare at his phone the whole ride, he looked around and opened himself up to the city that pulsed around him. Here he was, living in the greatest city in the world, and he never took the time to enjoy it. As the cab sat at a red light, Wyatt watched a couple, hand in hand, huddled close together against the cold. They had stopped in front of Saks Fifth Avenue to look at the window display, which featured an extravagant Christmas showcase every year. Along with the couple, a big crowd lurked in front of the window, which made it impossible for Wyatt to see this year's display. Come to think of it, he had never seen one of the displays. In all the years he had lived in New York City, he had never taken the time around the holidays to visit the tree at Rockefeller Center, gone to see the Rockettes Christmas Spectacular at Radio City Music Hall, or looked at the window displays at the large department stores like Saks, Bloomingdales or Leighton's.

Why was he suddenly getting sentimental about Christmas? It didn't take a genius to figure that one out. Isabella.

The ringing of his phone interrupted his thoughts. He looked down and saw his sister Alexa's name on the screen.

"Alexa, this must be a record—calling me twice in as many days."

"The real record is you answering twice," she teased.

"You got me there. Hey, have you ever been to see the Christmas window displays at any of the big department stores in the city?" There was silence on the line. "Alexa, are you there?"

"I'm here. I was looking down at my phone making sure I had called the right Wyatt. I don't think my brother Wyatt has ever asked me about Christmas window displays. Are you planning on going on a window display tour? If you are, I especially like Leighton's this year."

"Very funny. Forget about it. What can I help you with?"

"That's more like the Wyatt I know. Back to business."

"Right, right. I know. What's going on? Everything okay? Or are you calling to harass me some more about coming home for Christmas?"

"It's not harassment, it's more like repeated, loving reminders," Alexa laughed. "But I'm really calling, aside from strongly encouraging you to come home for Christmas, because I need your help."

"Okay, what's up?"

"You know how much Michael loves basketball, right?"

"Yeah, sure."

"The only thing Michael is asking for this Christmas is a basketball."

"That's easy. I can get him a basketball."

"I'm not finished. It's not just any basketball...he wants an autographed Damian Hawk basketball."

"As in Damian Hawk, the point guard for the New York Knicks?"

"That's the one!"

"Okay, and how do I fit into this?"

"Didn't you represent the owner of the Knick's last year when he was being sued?"

"Yes, I did represent Bill Kaftan," Wyatt didn't like where this was going.

"Do you think, maybe, you could ask him for a favor? Ask him to ask Damian to autograph a basketball for your nephew?"

Wyatt had reached his office now and having a conversation like this one at this early hour was giving him a headache. "I don't know, Alexa. I don't like to ask people for personal favors. Especially clients or former clients."

"You don't understand what this would mean to Michael! It is literally the only thing he's been talking about for weeks!"

"Did you try looking online for something? I'm sure you can buy an autographed basketball from most great players online."

"I tried. There are balls autographed from many other players, but the only one I found autographed by Damian Hawk—and I only found one—was thousands of dollars."

"Alexa, my schedule is crazy, I'm not sure I'll have time."

"Please Wyatt, I'm desperate! First imagine Michael's face when he opens that gift on Christmas morning. And then imagine his face if he doesn't get it. He'll be crushed. You know I wouldn't ask if it wasn't important."

Wyatt sighed and sat down in his chair, "I'll see what I can do."

"Thank you, thank you, thank you!" His sister squealed.

"Don't get your hopes up. It's still a longshot. And you haven't given me much time—Christmas is less than a week away!"

"I know. Okay." But it was too late for that; Alexa's hopes were already sky high.

"Can I get back to work now?"

"Of course. See you at Christmas!"

And before Wyatt could say another word, his sister hung up the phone. He had to give it to her, she was persistent. Wyatt pulled up his work calendar, and it was jam-packed with meetings and calls. Now, add hunting down both the owner of the New York Knicks and the top point guard in the NBA to his to-do list. The thought made him groan out loud.

Chapter Thirteen

The day wore on and Ella was in a distracted haze. She went through the motions, helping customers at the store, inserting the appropriate smile or nod when expected, but her heart wasn't in it. Her heart was full of an ache she didn't know was possible.

The pain and sorrow she suffered when her father passed away had been intense, she didn't know if she would ever feel happiness again. But as time moved on, that burning anguish dimmed to a dull twinge. It was always there, buried a little deeper with each passing day, but there, nonetheless.

However, this current brand of agony which consumed her was something altogether new. Thoughts of Wyatt had her eyes pleading for the next glance, her skin smoldering with anticipation of the next touch, and her heart longing for reciprocating love.

Sensing her mood, Marney surprised Ella with a caramel macchiato from the café across the street. Ella slowly sipped the warm, sweet caffeine without tasting a thing. During the quiet moments in the store, she studied without retaining a word. It was as if her body and brain were filled to the brim with a passionate yearning, and therefore had no capacity for anything else.

Her shift at The Book Nook ended like any other day and like no other day she had ever experienced. She reprimanded herself on her walk down to 430 Fifth Avenue, for letting a man get so far into her head that it became impossible for her to focus. And with a week of final exams ahead, she needed to get back on her game. Tonight's plan was to keep her head down and get the cleaning done at Dawson & Hancock as quickly and efficiently as possible, and then to go home and study for tomorrow's exam. However, even as she tried to re-center herself, she couldn't help but feel a thrill that she would spend the next few hours in Wyatt's office, so close yet so far away. Her life was suddenly one giant paradox.

Up on the 22nd floor she changed into her cleaning uniform and quickly scanned the office for any lights left on, signaling someone was still there working. Thankfully, the entire floor was dark and quiet. Rosie showed up on time and the two women got to work. Ella started in the bathrooms like she usually did, and Rosie started with the large offices. With Christmas love songs blasting through her earbuds, it wasn't long before Ella had finished cleaning the bathrooms and the cubicles. She went to check on Rosie and see if she needed any help. She found Rosie in an office that looked like the North Pole. Almost every square inch of the space was covered in faux snow, twinkle lights, life-size nutcrackers and even a giant inflatable snowman that Ella was pretty sure was meant to be an outdoor lawn ornament.

"Rosie!" She yelled over the sound of the vacuum. "Rosie!"

Rosie shut the vacuum off. "Look at all these pine needles! Can you believe this is only after one day! I'll tell you what, I can't wait for the holidays to be over."

"I'm done out there." She ignored Rosie's rant and pointed out the door toward the cubicle area. "Can I help you with anything?"

"No, I only have one office left. I'm okay. Go home. You look tired."

"Thanks, Rosie," she said, rolling her eyes.

"By the way, how was that fiesta over the weekend? Did you have a good time?"

Ella wasn't sure if she was more shocked by the fact that Rosie was asking her about her personal life or that she remembered that she'd gone to a party over the weekend. "It was fun, thanks for asking. Now, are you sure you don't want any help?"

"I'm fine! Shoo! Go." Rosie motioned for her to get out.

"Okay, I'm going! I'm going! Geez, only trying to help!"

Once Rosie heard the elevator ding signaling Ella had left the 22nd floor, she shimmied into the large corner office. She pulled a framed photo out of her bucket of cleaning supplies and placed it gently on the desk next to the computer. Stepping back, she admired her handiwork. Now this office had one framed photo in it. There was certainly no way he would miss it, since it was the *only* personal item in the whole room. A small giggle escaped her mouth as her little plan was coming together. Tomorrow, "New York City's Most Eligible Bachelor" would sit down in his chair, and there, staring back at him, would be Ella's sweet face.

Chapter Fourteen

Wyatt couldn't wait to get into the office, and it wasn't because he was excited to brief his team on their latest case. Nope, his newest client Mr. Beaman was not a thought on his mind. Beaman was being sued by a former employee. The employee slipped while walking down the stairs in the hotel Mr. Beaman owned, and was suing for an obscene amount of money. On a normal day, Wyatt would be pumped up with adrenaline to deal with a case like this one. This case was the epitome of why he became an attorney. But today, Mr. Beaman could have showed him video footage of the former employee faking the fall, and it would have barely registered on his radar.

The reason Wyatt rushed into his office early was to get an update from Marissa about Isabella's identity. He had gone over in his mind the different ways he planned to reach out to Isabella, and exactly what he would say to her. Currently he was oscillating between a laid-back approach, like simply sending her a text message, or a grand gesture, like showing up at the bookstore she worked at with flowers and tickets to go see the Rockettes Christmas show. That was one more thing he remembered about Isabella—she loved Christmas. He was leaning toward the grand gesture approach. 'Tis the season, right?

Once in his office, he hung up his overcoat, placed his briefcase on the floor next to his desk, and then froze. Sitting on his desk was a framed photo of he and Isabella from the newspaper. He looked around his office quickly, as if whoever put the picture there might still be in the room. He immediately picked up his phone and curtly asked Alice to step into his office.

In an instant Alice was poking her head into his office. "What can I help you with, Mr. Dawson? Would you like some coffee?"

"No. Well, yes." Wyatt shook his head trying to organize his thoughts. "Sorry. Let me try this again. Yes, I would love some coffee, however, that isn't what I wanted to ask you." He moved aside so Alice could see the photo on his desk. He looked at the photo and then back at her, without uttering a word.

"How nice, Mr. Dawson! You are finally adding some personal touches to your office! I have to admit, I always thought it was strange how you left your office so...empty."

He started shaking his head again, "No, Alice. That's not what I'm saying. I didn't put this here!" He pointed at the photo aggressively, as if he were afraid of it. "I was hoping you could tell me who *did* put it here! Someone came into my office and put this on my desk."

"Oh dear," Alice was more concerned with his reaction than the fact that someone had been in his office. "I have no idea, I'm afraid."

Wyatt's shoulders slumped in frustration.

"But if you don't mind me saying, I think it's lovely," she said as she smiled and looked at the photo again.

Exasperated, Wyatt opened his mouth to say something, and then changed his mind. "Could you get me some coffee, please."

Alice nodded, scurrying toward the door.

"Oh, and Alice, one more thing if you don't mind?"

She stopped and turned back toward him. "Yes?"

"Alexa called me today and asked that I help her with a Christmas gift for her oldest son, Michael. Could you try and get ahold of Bill Kaftan for me?"

"From the Knicks?"

"Yes. I can't believe I'm going to do this, but I need to ask him for a favor."

"Of course, Wyatt. He can be tough to get on the phone, but I'll see what I can do. For you, I think he'll take my call."

"Thank you, Alice. And the sooner the better. Christmas is less than a week away." Once Alice had left, he picked up the photo and moved it to the wooden shelf behind his desk. After a few deep breaths he turned on his computer. It was time to get to work. But first, he needed to call Marissa. She answered on the first ring.

"Marissa, it's Wyatt."

"Hi, Wyatt."

"Could you tell me what you learned about Isabella. Her last name, maybe? Who she came to the party with?"

The line was quiet for a beat. Wyatt almost spoke again, to be sure the line hadn't disconnected, but then Marissa spoke. Her normally strong, confident voice now sounded weak and soft. "I was planning on calling you about this, sir." She cleared her throat. "You see, I've had a bit of an issue learning much of anything about this Isabella."

"Well, what *have* you learned?"

More silence.

"Nothing?" Marissa spoke the word timidly, making it sound like a question rather than a statement.

"Nothing?"

"I'm afraid not."

"How is that possible? I thought you knew everyone at the party?"

"I did, too. But there is no one named Isabella listed as anyone's plus one. And we know she doesn't work for the firm."

"Are we sure she had an invitation?"

"She definitely had an invitation. They would not have let her through the two security checkpoints without one. That I know for sure."

"Well, she got an invitation from someone. I want you to ask every employee, both male and female, if they brought a woman named Isabella as their plus one."

"I did that, Wyatt."

"You already asked everyone? And no one brought her?"

113

"Yes. You now understand why I didn't get back to you yesterday. I don't have any information yet."

"It's as if she didn't really exist, like she was some kind of angel who descended down to earth for the party and disappeared back to the heavens before saying goodbye." Wyatt's voice sounded wistful.

Marissa couldn't believe that this was Wyatt Dawson she was speaking to. "Don't worry," she said. "I haven't given up yet."

Fidgeting with his desk drawer, he saw something sparkle on his desk as the sunlight landed on its flat surface. He took the gold pendant in his hand.

"Did you hear me, sir? I haven't given up yet."

"Right, yes, thank you, Marissa. She's got to be missing her necklace. I know her father gave it to her," he added, thinking out loud.

"Did you say necklace?" Marissa's voice gained strength.

"Yeah, why?"

"What else do you know about the necklace?"

Wyatt could hear her brain working. "Her father gave it to her, and it really meant a lot to her," he said.

"What else do you know about her father? Do you know his name? Anything?"

"If I knew his name we wouldn't be in this situation, would we?"

"Right." Marissa was quiet, thinking.

"And it wouldn't matter, anyway."

"What do you mean? What wouldn't matter?"

"You wouldn't be able to find her father, he passed away years ago."

"I'm going to work on this, sir. I've got an idea." Marissa sounded confident and determined.

"Okay, thanks Marissa. This means a lot to me. I'm going to keep calling bookstores—maybe I'll get lucky."

"Bookstores? Why are you calling bookstores?"

"Isabella works at a bookstore."

"This is what I need you to do," Marissa dictated. "You need to email me a list of every little thing you know about this woman. I want to know every tiny detail, however insignificant it might appear."

"Consider it done."

Chapter Fifteen

After another fitful night of sleep, Ella was surviving on coffee alone. At least today she made it to her exam on time. Once there, however, she found it hard to concentrate on the actual test. Thankfully after years of focused study in her major, she knew the material well and although she might not get an A on the test, she knew she had answered enough correctly to get a C or maybe even a B. She'd take it. This was the last test that would go this way, she promised herself. The rest of the week she had to get back on track.

After her exam, Ella listened to a voicemail that had come in while she'd been taking the test. It was a message from Marney, who babbled on for a what seemed like ten minutes. From what Ella could surmise the store was quiet, and Ella shouldn't bother coming in to work unless she wanted to because she needed the money. But Marney thought she should do something fun instead. Ella was going to miss The Book Nook.

For Ella's "fun" afternoon, she decided to go to the community center to see how Bonnie was doing. Amid all the recent events, Ella had forgotten about the staff at the center, especially Bonnie, who as Executive Director would not only lose contact with all the children but lose her job as well. Ella could really use a little bit of Christmas spirit right now. The expression "when it rains, it pours," came to mind as she opened the doors to the center. Exams, a lost necklace, her last few weeks working at The Book Nook, the

Kate Kasch

community center closing…and a broken heart. There were too many changes happening all at once.

With a deep sigh, Ella slapped on a happy face and bounced into the main stage area, ready to face the kids. They must have been working hard over the weekend, because the stage looked like a Christmas wonderland. At stage right there stood a giant, lush Christmas tree, adoringly lop-sided. Red and gold tinsel was unevenly wrapped around the tree; it was bunched up in some spots, leaving other areas completely bare. Homemade ornaments hung from the pine branches. More were placed on the lower branches of the tree, fewer in the middle, and almost no ornaments at the top. It reminded her of the red ombre dress. It was perfect. A single tear slid down her cheek as she gazed at the tree.

Stage left was filled with towering cardboard cutouts painted, most likely by the older kids, to look like the interior of an office. Scrooge's office, no doubt. There were two wooden desks, each with a mismatched chair. Above the larger desk, a sign was hanging that read, "TIME IS MONEY." When Ella pictured Scrooge's office in her mind it was dark and gray and dreary, but the kids had clearly used some artistic license because the stage was full of color. It was the happiest looking office Scrooge would ever see.

"Ella!" Joana ran toward her at full speed, her curly ponytail bouncing and large dark eyes bright and wide. Before she could stop her, Joana knocked into her and wrapped her arms around her neck. Ella laughed. It felt good.

"Joana!" Ella hugged her back. "You look very festive today!" Joana was wearing a bright red sweater with giant gold and white pom poms sewed onto it.

"Isn't it great?" She asked excitedly. "We're making sweaters for the finale of the show. You know, at the end when we all come back onto the stage and we bow and everyone in the audience claps and whistles and tells us how amazing we are?"

Ella laughed again. "I can't wait to clap and whistle! This show is going to be epic!" She and Joana fist bumped.

"You should see all the things we have to decorate our sweaters with! There are sequins and buttons and tinsel and pipe cleaners and…want to help me add some bling to my sweater?"

Ella knew it was a good idea to come here today.

Elbow deep in sequins, she felt a tap on her shoulder and turned around to see Bonnie. Bonnie was in her standard uniform of khakis and a polo shirt with the center's logo embroidered on it. Despite Bonnie's smile as she watched the crew of kids decorating their sweaters, her ice blue eyes were wet with tears. Christmas songs were streaming through a small portable speaker, kids were singing and chatting cheerfully as they glued and glittered. But with one simple look at her, Ella could see Bonnie's heart breaking.

Without speaking, Bonnie signaled Ella to follow her, away from the group of kids. After brushing sequins and glitter off her hands and her sweater, she followed.

"Is everything okay?" Ella asked as soon as they were out of earshot of the kids.

"Well, not really." Bonnie wasn't one to beat around the bush. She ran her hand through her short, gray hair, her face pinched with worry. "You understand the situation the center is in, right?"

"You mean, that you lost your sponsorship money and you only have until the end of the year to come up with an alternative source of funds?"

Bonnie nodded. "It seems that's not our only problem. The Christmas show is Thursday night, only two days away, and we have an issue with the costumes."

"I don't understand. I thought the kids made their own costumes?"

"They did, and they were wonderful. The kids were so proud of them," Bonnie's voice cracked.

"What do you mean, they *were* wonderful?"

"They're gone," Bonnie whispered. Was she worried about the kids hearing her or were the words too hard to utter out loud?

"How can they be gone? You mean, like someone stole them? Who would steal from a children's community center? And who would want a bunch of handmade costumes for a Christmas play?"

Bonnie shook her head, "No. The costumes weren't stolen. We had a bunch of bags full of donated clothes we had collected that were being sent to a children's charity. The families here donated old coats and hats, that kind of thing. We had a clothing drive going for months. The charity came to pick up the bags of donations a few days ago, and well, the bags of costumes were near the other bags. The charity took everything."

"I'm sure you can get the costume bags back. Did you call the charity?"

"I called them, but they've had a lot of trucks going around picking up donations all over the city and the tri-state area. They have no way to track where our donated goods ended up."

Ella's eyes got big as the gravity of the situation sank in. It had taken weeks to make those costumes. The play was in two days. They wouldn't even have any more fabric or old clothing to work with—everything had been second-hand or donated.

"Oh, my goodness, Bonnie. What are you going to do?"

Bonnie's eyes filled with tears and her voice shook with desperation, "I don't know! I can't tell the kids that all those costumes they worked for hours creating, are gone. And then, to tell them only a few days later that the center is closing its doors…it's too much. For many of them, this place is their safe haven. It's the only place between a straight path and a path that leads to the streets! Oh, Ella! What am I going to do?"

Ella took a deep breath. Suddenly her own problems seemed small in comparison. "Don't tell anyone anything. I'll think of something," she said with more confidence than she felt.

The next few hours Ella went through the motions of helping the boys and girls decorate their sweaters, which she learned from Bonnie was an activity to distract them from the missing costumes. When not one square inch of sweater could be seen underneath all the decorations, the Christmas music was turned down and the schoolbooks came out. The kids sat at the long rectangular table with their books out and heads down in concentration. Ella made her way down the row of girls and boys, pausing to ask each child if they needed any help. Although the dancing and game-playing was always fun, this part of the day was her favorite. This was when she felt she was adding value and making a difference, however clichéd that might sound.

Pausing next to Joana, Ella asked her if she needed any help.

"No, my homework is easy-peasy. I already finished it. I'm working on writing a story. Miss Bonnie says if we finish our work early, then we need to find something quiet to do so we don't disturb anyone else. I've been writing short stories."

Ella looked over the girl's shoulder at her paper. "What is your story about? You've already written pages full!"

"The title of the story is *The Christmas Dress*," Joana said, smiling proudly. "I wanted to combine my passions of fashion and Christmas!"

Ella returned the smile. "I've always known you were a fashionista. I think you should draw the art for the cover of your story."

"I did!" Joana pulled a piece of paper out from under the one she was writing on. She had used markers to draw a woman with long, dark hair wearing a floor length red gown. With a silver glitter marker, she had made the dress sparkle.

"Joana, that drawing is amazing! You are quite the talent!"

"It's you!" Joana laughed.

"What do you mean, it's me?"

"I drew a picture of you wearing a sparkly red dress. You were my inspiration."

"I'm honored," Ella said, putting her hands to her heart. "I actually have a red Christmas dress, and it is the most amazing dress I've ever owned."

"No way! I love wearing red at Christmastime." Joana looked at her drawing.

"Wait a minute!" Ella said, "My dress! I think I have an idea!" Her mind went into overdrive coming up with a plan. "Joana, I need to go. Can you tell Miss Bonnie I had to leave?"

Joana smiled and nodded rapidly, sensing the change in Ella's demeanor as she went from hopeless to determined.

"And tell her not to worry about a thing—I have a plan!"

As soon as Ella was outside the community center, she walked south toward the subway station at a brisk pace. As she walked, she tried repeatedly to call Marney's phone, with no success. *Oh Marney, why aren't you answering your phone?* The Book Nook phone line was a continual busy signal, which was odd. And frustrating. There was only one thing to do. She tucked her phone back into her bag and rushed down the stairs to the subway platform. If she couldn't get Marney on the phone, she was going to have to go to The Book Nook and ask for the favor in person.

As she burst through the front door of the bookstore, cold air collided with warm air, forming a tornado-like gust of energy. The eruption received attention from both Marney and her customers, who were all surprised by the outburst in the typically quiet, calm space. Ella's fiery eyes locked with Marney's, whose eyebrows were raised in either shock or curiosity—most likely a little of both.

Gathering her wits, Ella forced a smile and said polite "hellos" to the handful of customers browsing the book aisles. Marney watched her as she attempted a relaxed, albeit rushed walk through the store.

"I need a favor," Ella blurted out in a loud whisper the moment she was close enough for Marney to hear her. Unfortunately, Marney was known for many things, but good hearing was not one of them. She leaned toward Ella with her hand cupped to her ear, signaling for her to speak up.

"*I need a favor!*" Ella yelled.

Marney held up a finger as she finished checking out a customer, and then they escaped to the back room.

"All this excitement! I haven't seen you look this alive in days, Ella!" Marney was practically jumping up and down. Ignoring the comment, Ella jumped right into an explanation of the situation at the Manhattan Community Center.

"No costumes? The poor children! What are they going to do?"

"That's where we come in," Ella said. "I have an idea, but I'm going to need your help."

After a few hours spent putting their plan into action, Ella glanced down at her phone and saw the time.

"Oh, my goodness! I had no idea it was this late. I need to go clean!"

"Go, go! I will finish up here!"

Ella hugged Marney tightly and rushed out the door and down to 430 Fifth Avenue. She spent the walk going over her plan, trying to find anything that could go wrong. The whole idea was a little bit crazy and a long shot for sure, but she had faith it would work out. It had to.

The night of cleaning went by with no issues. No run-ins with any employees of Dawson & Hancock or any other problems. Strangely, Rosie had asked that they swap their usual duties, so Ella was cleaning the large offices tonight which was a nice change. As she walked into the last office to clean—the large office that she and Rosie had jokingly referred to as "Scrooge's office,"something on the desk caught Ella's attention.

Sitting on the desk between the computer mouse and the phone was a framed photograph. *Scrooge does have a heart,* Ella thought to herself. Curiosity got the better of her and she picked up the frame to get a better look at the photo. She gasped! With her breath caught in her throat and her stomach a flurry of nerves, she stared at the photo. It was the one from the newspaper of Wyatt and Isabella.

Did he frame this and put it here? Does this mean this is his office? Scrooge's office is Wyatt's office? Wyatt is Scrooge? Her mind was racing, and her legs felt like they could no longer hold the weight of her body. She plopped herself down in the office chair, Wyatt's chair, and carefully placed the frame back down on the desk. As she looked around the office with fresh eyes and a new perspective, she still found it hard to reconcile the warm, kind man she spent time with at the dance with this cold office space. The night of the party he confessed to being a workaholic, why wouldn't he want his office to be a comforting place? Something was not adding up. She wished she could ask him.

Once her legs felt like they would work again, Ella stood and started to clean up. With each swipe of her cloth or whisk of her duster she felt a surge of connection as she imagined his hands gracing the very same spot. She found herself moving slowly, savoring every inch of the office. As she washed the windows and looked out over the city lights below, she was reminded of how she and Wyatt had sat together on the roof of the building taking in this very same view. It was only two nights ago, but it might as well have been an eternity.

Chapter Sixteen

Another restless night, and another final exam down the tubes. Ella felt like a zombie as she walked to The Book Nook. She should have been devastated. She should have been angry and disappointed in herself. Instead, she felt numb. When she did sleep, her dreams were filled with strange theatrical plays starring Wyatt and Joana and an old man, who pointed a bent, shaking finger at Ella and chastised her for failing her classes. She woke up tangled in sweaty sheets, her heart racing. A pounding headache crept in as she rushed to get dressed, and it stayed with her all the way through her exam.

And now she was dazed and detached. All these years of trying to hold it all together. To be there for her mom, to get straight A's in school, to work two jobs to pay for school, and to volunteer with kids to try and make a difference. And what did it get her? She was alone. She had no friends, no boyfriend, and possibly no degree if she continued to do poorly on her finals. And to top it all off, the community center was closing, abandoning all those children who relied on it for support and guidance. What was the point of it all?

Out of habit she reached up to her neck to hold her gold pendant, to summon her father's spirit for support. As she felt around her naked neck, the realization that the necklace was gone came down on her hard. It was as if she was experiencing the shock of the loss all over again. This missing necklace—this was why her heart felt heavy and her mind was filled with negativity. She no longer had her father with her.

"Oh my! Look what the Grinch dragged in," Marney exclaimed when Ella walked through the front door of The Book Nook. "Isabella! I have never seen you like this. Did something else happen?"

Ella trudged in and dropped her heavy book bag on the front counter with a thud. "You mean aside from me failing my classes, probably not getting my degree, disappointing children I care about and losing a cherished family heirloom? Um, no, I think that about covers it."

"This isn't the Ella that I know. Where's the positive spin? Where's the 'glass half full' girl I know and love?"

"Now I feel guilty about letting you down, too!" Ella whined. She took off her coat and scarf and sighed. "I'm sorry, Marney. I'm having a hard time seeing the good in my life right now. But I don't' mean to take it out on you."

Marney wrapped Ella in a hug. "Oh, honey. It's all going to work out, I promise." She pulled away from Ella, but kept her hands on Ella's arms, looking her in the eyes. "I understand you're going through a challenging time right now. But the ups and downs in life…they are proof that you're *living!* You have spent years going through the motions. But now, now you're challenging yourself! Putting yourself out there! Experiencing new things!"

Ella's eyes filled with tears, and she looked down at her hands.

"These lows that you're experiencing, they make the highs that much sweeter. I promise."

"Thanks, Marney. What would I do without you?"

The phone rang and Marney ran to the back to answer it. Merry waltzed over toward Ella and put his head on her lap. She absentmindedly stroked his soft fur.

"I know what will cheer you up!" Marney came rushing back to the front of the store, her magenta and yellow silk tunic swishing as she moved. Ella looked up at her without saying a word, continuing to stroke Merry's head.

"Remember that little plan of yours to help the children and the Christmas play at the community center?"

Ella managed a nod.

"I just got off the phone, and it's a go!"

"Really? They said yes?"

Marney nodded, a wide smile spreading on her face.

Ella jumped up and grabbed Marney in a hug. "Marney! This is amazing! Thank you!"

"Oh, it's nothing," Marney scoffed, waving her off.

"Are you kidding? It's everything! Okay, what's the plan?"

"They're going to meet us at the community center tomorrow morning."

"The play is tomorrow night."

"I know. They think they can pull it together in a day."

"What time tomorrow morning?" Ella asked, trying to figure out a timeline.

"Early. 8 a.m."

Ella started pacing. "8 a.m. Okay, I will make it work."

"Do you have another exam tomorrow?"

"I do. It's my last one," Ella said. "It's at ten. I will come to the community center at eight, stay for an hour and a half, run down to school to take my exam, and then go back up to the center."

"Are you sure you can swing that? That sounds like a tight timeline—everything is pretty far away from each other. And remember, your exam comes first."

Ella nodded quickly. "I can do it. I have to make this work."

With her spirits slightly lifted, Ella immersed herself in work at the store. She advised customers and gave out lollipops to children. Being able to forget about her own problems for a while was sheer bliss. Before she knew it, her shift at the bookstore was over and it was time to go to 430 Fifth Avenue to clean.

Chapter Seventeen

Upon receiving the email from Wyatt which detailed all intel on the mysterious Isabella, Marissa Mulvaney was confident she could quickly discover the woman's full identity. Using her large whiteboard, she started a chart highlighting all the important information she now knew. She combined that with what she learned from the eccentric "assistant" that came in asking for the gold necklace, and she had…well, not much.

> **Initials are ILM – Isabella?**
> **Owns a white cashmere coat and a gold pendant**
> **Father has passed away**
> **Works at a bookstore somewhere in NYC**
> **Studying to be teacher at NYU**
> **Volunteers at a community center in NYC**
> **Assistant Regina White (alias?)**

Wyatt had started by calling bookstores, but that was too tedious for Marissa. The most obvious place to start, in her mind, was NYU. At her computer, she did a search for "NYU and Isabella." After scrolling through the first few pages of the 400,000 links, Marissa quickly realized that wasn't getting her anywhere. She realized that there was one little fact in the email Wyatt had sent her that she hadn't added to her white board. The community center Isabella worked at was performing a Christmas play sometime soon. This time Marissa searched for "community center Christmas play New York City." Bingo. The third link was for The Manhattan Community Center in Harlem. It was performing, according to their website, a fun and wild take on "A Christmas Carol." And the play was tomorrow night.

Normally, when she knew she was onto something, her heart would race. But right now, her heart was sprinting like there was a shoe sale on Louboutin's and there was only one pair left in her size. She picked up her phone and dialed the number to the Manhattan Community Center.

"The Manhattan Community Center, how can I help you?" a weathered, yet cheery, woman's voice came through the line.

"Hello! I hope you can help me. I was wondering if an Isabella works at the Community Center?"

"No, we don't have an Isabella that works here, you must have the wrong place."

Marissa's heart sank. She was sure this was the right place.

"Oh, I was trying to find a certain woman. She's young, very pretty, with dark hair...anyway, she lost a necklace and I wanted to find her and return it."

"George!" The woman on the line yelled so loudly, Marissa had to move the phone away from her ear. "Sorry. Hold on a sec," she said, now speaking to Marissa again.

"George! Is Ella's full name Isabella?" she yelled again. Despite the high decibel, Marissa didn't pull the phone away from her ear this time. This time she listened as closely as she could, straining to hear whatever information George had to offer.

"That's what I thought," the woman said away from the phone. "Hi, ma'am, we do have an Ella, her real name is Isabella, she doesn't work here, but she volunteers. Could that be who you're looking for?"

Marissa's heart soared. "Yes! Yes, I think that's her! Is she there right now?"

"Oh, no. No, sorry. She's not here right now but she should be back sometime later today or maybe tomorrow morning. It all depends."

"Depends on what?"

"It all depends on what time her final exam is today, and also what time she gets off work at the bookstore."

Ah ha! Marissa had found her. "And what bookstore is that? Maybe I could try and reach her there."

After a few more yells to George, the woman came back with the answer. Marissa grabbed her coat and her bag and headed for the elevator. She was on her way to The Book Nook to finally meet Isabella, aka "Ella," Martinez. And the store was only ten blocks away. Looking at her phone, she saw the time and was worried because the store would be closing soon. This was her chance to find Ella, and she wasn't going to miss it. She had to hurry.

The sidewalks were packed with groups of pedestrians shuffling slowly past storefronts, admiring Christmas displays. Fingers were pointing at twinkling lights and signs announcing sales. Tourists, including couples and families, stopped to take the requisite photos of themselves in New York City so they could boast on social media about their trip. Despite the cold, there were smiles on everyone's faces. Marissa charged by these joyous people, her face set with determination. Expertly weaving through the crowds, she walked briskly and with purpose. She could already hear the excitement in Wyatt's voice when she told him she had found Isabella. Despite being anxious to tell him, she was waiting until she was one hundred percent positive Ella Martinez was indeed Isabella.

A few storefronts away from The Book Nook Marissa's body became a flurry of nerves. What if Ella wanted nothing to do with Wyatt? What if she had a boyfriend—or a husband? Her mind raced with last-minute doubts. The Book Nook was now one store away. She steeled herself against her apprehensions and prepared to meet Isabella. A young woman was walking out of the bookstore and there was something in the way the woman moved that caused Marissa to pause mid-step.

Ducking behind a planter holding a twinkle-light covered bush, Marissa watched the woman leave the store. The woman's dark hair was pulled back in a high bun and she wore very little makeup. However, there was something about the long, graceful stride and the beautiful olive skin that confirmed Marissa's initial instinct. It was Ella Martinez. For reasons not immediately known to Marissa, she started following Ella down the block instead of approaching her. Clad entirely in black, Ella was easy to lose in the sea of black that is the sidewalk of New York City, however, the sheer volume of pedestrians gave Marissa plenty of cover. Thankfully, Ella didn't appear to be in much of a rush and Marissa was able to keep her in her sights.

Ella walked south, down the same sidewalk that Marissa had just walked up. Marissa took the opportunity to study Ella. She noticed the young woman didn't glance at the Christmas décor in the storefront windows and she didn't smile at the couple taking a selfie on the corner. Ella looked forward but didn't seem to notice anything going on around her. She was either lost in her own thoughts or made this walk down Fifth Avenue so frequently that her body was on autopilot. Perhaps it was a little bit of both.

Suddenly Ella stopped in front of a building and went in. Marissa looked up and was shocked to see where she now stood. They were at 430 Fifth Avenue. Would Ella be going into this building? Did she work here, too? Marissa looked down at her phone and saw that it was 8 p.m. Most of the offices in this building would be closed by now. She waited a beat and then followed Ella in.

Ella walked up to the security desk and laughed with the guard on duty. Based on their banter and easy smiles, it was clear the two were familiar with one another. Marissa stayed toward the front doors of the building, and subtly held up her phone as if she were reading a text. She took a photo of Ella and the guard talking. Once Ella was through security and walking toward the elevator bank, Marissa briskly walked through the lobby. She did her best to move quickly without bringing any attention to herself. She flashed her badge to security and cautiously approached the elevator bank area.

The problem, Marissa surmised, was that Ella would recognize her if they came into contact. At this point she was intrigued by Ella being in this building and wanted to see what the mystery woman was up to before revealing herself. This late in the evening, the elevator bank area would be almost empty. She felt like a spy in a James Bond movie as she inched her way along the wall leading toward the elevators. She stopped at the corner, took a deep breath, and poked her head around the corner to take in the situation at the elevator bank. Much to her shock and dismay, it was empty. She had missed her. With over thirty floors in the building, there was no way to find out where Ella was going. Except...

Marissa rushed back to the security desk. She plastered a wide smile on her face, straightened her jacket, and sauntered over to the guard Ella had been chatting with. He was large and bald, with a friendly demeanor.

"Hello there! How are you tonight?"

Jacob smiled in his easy way. "I'm good, now. How are you, ma'am? Is there something I can help you with?"

"Actually, there is—" she said, looking at his nametag. "Jacob."

Nodding slowly, Jacob eyed her skeptically. He had watched her come through security many times, and she had never said hello or even glanced up in his direction. And now suddenly she's smiling and calling him by name. What was it she was after?

"I was hoping you could help me. You know that young woman you were talking to, Ella?"

Jacob froze. He wasn't about to confirm or deny whether he knew Ella. Ella was one of the highlights of his shift. He knew she worked long days, and still she always stopped and said hello and asked about his family. Tonight she asked what Nina, his six-year-old little girl, wanted for Christmas. If this blonde woman was looking to cause Ella any trouble, she was looking in the wrong place.

Ivy league degrees were part of Marissa's resume, but that wasn't what made her good at her job. The thing that made Marissa good—great, actually—at her job was that she understood people. She knew she had never made eye contact or said hello to this security guard despite having him check her badge on many occasions. She also realized he took a defensive stance when she mentioned Ella's name, and that he was prepared to protect her. In seconds, Marissa had processed all this information and devised a new approach.

"Actually, I don't know her name," she continued. "I think it's Ella Martinez. She dropped a gold necklace with the initials ILM on it when she was at a Christmas party a few nights ago, and I want to get it back to her. Could you tell me where she works? Or even what floor she works on?"

Jacob paused and studied Marissa's face. Could he trust her? He did know Ella's last name was Martinez, and he felt he could remember her frequently reaching up around her neck to play with some type of gold pendant. In the end, his desire to help Ella overpowered his skepticism of the blonde.

"Sure," he said, nodding. "She works on the 22nd floor. Wyatt & Dawson."

Marissa's chin dropped to her chest, but then realized the guard must be mistaken. She shook her head no. "No, that can't be. She can't work for Wyatt & Dawson."

"Well, she's not a lawyer or anything like that. She does the cleaning."

"You mean she's part of the night cleaning crew? Like, a maid?"

"I don't think people say 'maid' anymore, but yeah. That's why I'm not sure you have the right person. I don't think Ella would have been at any Christmas party. Not any Christmas party *you'd* be at, anyway."

And just like that, everything clicked.

In a daze, Marissa left the office building and hailed a cab home. She needed time to process this new information. As if he could sense her apprehension, the moment she sat down in the cab, Wyatt called her on her cell phone. She contemplated ignoring the call but knew he would most likely keep trying her until she answered.

"Hi, Wyatt!" she tried to keep her voice cheery.

"Marissa, hi! I apologize for calling this late, but I wanted to know if you made any progress trying to find Isabella." He was trying to sound professional, but to Marissa he seemed desperate and impatient. In other words, he sounded like he was in love.

"It's no problem, you know you can call me anytime." She paused a beat. "I have made some progress and have a new lead, but I want to confirm it before I tell you anything."

"Wow, that sounds really promising! Thank you, Marissa." He couldn't stop himself from continuing. "Tomorrow then. You'll update me tomorrow." It wasn't a question.

"Of course. Wyatt?"

"What is it, Marissa?"

"What if we find Isabella and she's not who you think she is? What if she's different than she appeared at the Christmas party?"

He was quiet. "Is there something you want to tell me, Marissa?"

"No! No, of course not. I don't want you to be disappointed, that's all."

She could hear him sigh. "I'm not sure what you mean by different. But, want to know what I *am* sure about? I'm sure that talking with Isabella that night was like no other conversation I've ever had with a woman in my life. I'm sure that we were meant to meet. I'm sure that she's kind, and intelligent and beautiful. She listens and she's honest. That's what I *am* sure about."

When Marissa heard the word "honest" she cringed. She was pretty sure Isabella had been anything but honest with Wyatt on the night they met. Maybe that wasn't even the first time they met—maybe Ella orchestrated the whole encounter in order to meet "New York City's Most Eligible Bachelor"? Who knows what tricks Isabella used to deceive Wyatt and make him fall for her?

Panic was rising in Marissa's body. This was all her fault and now it was her job to protect Wyatt from this opportunistic woman. And what would the press say about this relationship if they got hold of the information? It would look terrible for the firm. Tomorrow she would tell Wyatt that she couldn't find Isabella, and she would somehow convince him to stop looking. The only option was to make sure he and Isabella never saw each other again.

Chapter Eighteen

Thursday morning was December 22nd, the day of the Christmas show at the community center. Ella woke up full of energy at 5 a.m. and her mind was already swirling like the snow in a shaken snow globe. As she went through her plan to help the children at the center, she closed her eyes and prayed for it all to work out. Her stomach was a ball of nerves and she couldn't eat breakfast, but she stopped at a café on the way into the city and treated herself to a mocha latte. The caffeine would give her that extra push she needed to get through the hectic day ahead.

It was still dark when Ella stepped outside. Overnight, the temperature had dropped at least ten degrees and the wind was whipping through the city streets. On her way to the train station, she pulled her scarf tightly around her neck. The wind pushed down on her making it hard for her to lift her head up. But it wasn't snowing, and for this she was grateful. There were a few deliveries expected at the community center today, and snow could derail those plans.

She got to the center around six and was the first to arrive. Fortunately, Bonnie had given her the passcode to unlock the doors. When she heard the click of the lock disengaging, she took a deep breath and pushed her way inside. It was time.

Ella shivered in the dark, cold auditorium as she turned on lights and bumped up the heat. Without the children's chatter and laughter, the space was eerily quiet. She kept moving in order to create some noise, which also helped to keep her from being spooked. She almost laughed out loud as she realized that if this were the "A Christmas Carol" movie, this would be the perfect time for her to be visited by one of the Christmas ghosts. She decided that if she had her pick, she would prefer the Ghost of Christmas Future. That way she would know how everything turned out and could stop worrying about it all. A flash of Wyatt's dashing smile filled her mind and she quickly tried to push it away and think about something else.

A chime rang through the center, and she rushed to the front door. As she opened it, Marney stood there looking like a Christmas tree in her bright red coat and green scarf. A giant smile lit up her face and she jumped up and down, waving at Ella. Relief flooded over Ella. Now she wouldn't have to be alone in the creepy center and help had arrived!

After a quick hug, Ella asked, "Have you heard anything? Is everything still good to go?"

Marney nodded, and recognizing Ella's nervous energy asked her, "How much coffee have you had, dear?"

"There isn't enough coffee in New York City to get me through today. What time are they supposed to get here?"

"Any minute now. In the meantime, why don't you show me around?"

Ella walked Marney through the center. She pointed out the coat room, storage facilities, the stage, and the backstage. "I thought this larger room right here," Ella said as they entered one of the rooms backstage, "would be a good place to lay out all the fabric so we can see what we have." She pointed to two adjoining rooms. "And these two can be used for changing rooms. One for the girls and one for the boys."

"They're quite small," Marney said, as she peeked through the doors.

"That's because they were originally storage closets," Ella replied. "This is a community center in Harlem, Marney, not a Broadway theater in Midtown."

"I'm thinking out loud, that's all. We'll make it work, of course."

A bell chimed again, echoing through the auditorium. Ella and Marney stopped in their tracks and looked at each other with wide eyes.

"They're here," Ella said, her body suddenly frozen still.

Marney nodded and smiled. "We should probably go let them in!"

The two women rushed to the front of the building and opened the front doors. The space instantly came alive with chatter and warmth as the glam squad burst through the doors. Ella clasped her hands together under her chin, tears springing to her eyes. Help had arrived.

Ella recognized Angela, Donny and Jessie, the three who helped pick out her dress for the Christmas party. They were all pulling suitcases on wheels behind them with one hand and had bags draped over their shoulders and in their free hands. Jackie, the queen of hair styling with her black-rimmed glasses and rainbow hair in a high ponytail, came over and air-kissed Ella on both cheeks. She was followed by Mac, the beautifully bald makeup guru. Although she had only met the squad one time, it felt like family was walking through the doors of the center. Now that the team was here, Ella knew everything was going to work out.

Liana Lapierre was the last to enter. She wore a black coat that cinched at her small waist and then flared out wide, reminding Ella of a structured tutu. Not a hair was out of place and her signature red lipstick, which would look ridiculous on anyone else at six in the morning, finished off the look. Despite the early hour and the frigid temperatures, she was still the definition of chic.

"I saw your photo in the paper," Liana said as she, too, air-kissed both of Ella's cheeks. "It's a shame you were wearing a tuxedo jacket over my gown."

Ella's eyebrows raised and she was stunned into silence. She hadn't thought about who else may have seen the photo in the paper. "I'm sorry," she stammered. "But I had no idea anyone even took my photo, otherwise I certainly would have given you credit."

"Oh, don't be silly, Isabella. If I were in the arms of that beau, I wouldn't know what was going on around me either," she winked as she spoke, and Ella blushed like a teenager.

Ella brought out the few articles of clothing that the Center still had, and she stood on a chair and talked to the whole group about the play. She explained the extensive creative liberties the children had taken on the original *A Christmas Carol*. This version was full of color, and Ella asked the squad to grab inspiration from the set design. She then handed out a full list of the characters in the play, and the age of the child playing that character.

After a quick tour of the auditorium and makeshift backstage, Liana took control. Like a conductor at an orchestra, she created a flow within her directions which her crew followed with a graceful rhythm. The characters were divvyed up between the squad members, and even Marney and Ella were responsible for the creation of one or two costumes. Ella reminded everyone to keep it simple, this was not a Broadway show. The kids would love anything they were given. The crew unloaded fabrics from silks to faux leather to cotton and faux fur, all in a rainbow of colors. There were large containers overflowing with buttons, zippers, feathers and sequins.

Upbeat Christmas music blasted through the sound system, creating a festive mood. Ella ordered donuts, muffins and coffee to be delivered and Liana's squad nibbled on treats while they cut, sewed and glued. It was the perfect balance of focus and fun. The last few days had been stressful. This was the first time Ella had the opportunity to relax and enjoy some Christmas cheer.

Ella was deeply focused on creating the Ghost of Christmas Present's wildly colorful costume and she lost track of time. Marney came running up to her, flushed from the exertion. "Ella, don't you have a final exam this morning?"

Jumping up from her seat and upsetting a large bowl of buttons that crashed to the floor with a startling bang, Ella screeched out a noise that was somewhere between a groan and a scream.

"Is everything okay, Ella?" Jackie asked, her rainbow hair glowing under the lights.

Ella felt sick with panic. "Oh my gosh, not again! How did I do this again?" She looked at her phone, it was 9:50 a.m. Her final was at ten o'clock and it was all the way downtown. She would never make it on time. Zigzagging her way through piles of fabric, an ironing board, and costumes laid out all over the floor, she raced to the cubby room. She shoved her arms through her coat, grabbed her bookbag and was out the front door of the building in seconds.

Outside, her mind did a quick calculation of the fastest way to get to downtown Manhattan. She could take a cab but would risk getting stuck traffic. But if the streets were clear, it would be the fastest. She could run to the subway, or she could take a bus. The bus was out, she thought. Too many stops. Cab or subway? She couldn't risk getting stuck in traffic. She had to take the subway.

That decision was made in her mind in a matter of seconds, and she sprinted down the street to the 125th Street subway station. Thankfully, the downtown A Train was pulling up to the platform as she pushed her way through the turnstile. She ran and slipped through the doors of the train right as they were closing. This train car was a newer one, and it had a map of the stops lit up on the interior wall of the car. It was torture watching the little blinking light slowly move from stop to stop. She refused to look at her phone; it would only cause her to panic more and there was no way for her to get to her test any faster.

Finally, the train stopped at West 4th Street Station and Ella raced onto the platform and up the stairs onto the street. The walk from that station to her class at NYU usually took her about six minutes but today, at a full-on sprint, she made it in about half that. She paused for a few seconds at the classroom door, caught her breath, and then opened the door as quietly as possible. A quick glance at the clock inside the room showed it was 10:15. She prayed Professor Scanlon would allow her to take the exam.

After a stern warning, Professor Scanlon handed Ella the exam. He told her she had forty-five minutes left. She'd better get started. Relief flooded her body as she sank into the first empty seat she found. She did her best to focus on the questions, but her brain was scattered like Legos in a playroom and she had to reread sentences multiple times. In the essay section, she felt like she could barely put a thought together.

When the bell rang and time was up, Ella felt defeated. It was as if her body was so full of dismay, it became too heavy to move. Reluctantly, she handed in her test and then trudged out of the classroom. She was leaving in a manner completely opposite from the way she came in. From filled with adrenaline, to filled with dread.

On the subway ride back uptown to the Community Center, Ella was in a daze. She had finished what might be her last final exam ever, and she should have been filled with a gleeful sense of accomplishment. Liberated and free. Instead, she chastised herself and thought about how disappointed her father would have been.

If she failed, all the money and time she had spent would be for nothing. She would have to spend even more money—money she didn't have—to pay for another whole semester of school. It would delay her ability to apply for teaching positions. She had a plan; a well-thought-out plan which she kept on a spreadsheet saved on her laptop. That spreadsheet gave her focus and comfort—it helped remind her that she wasn't flailing in the wind. She was driven. And now she felt like she had driven right off a cliff. Never again. Out of habit, she reached up to her neck to grab hold of her pendant, and tears sprung to her eyes. It was the end of the week, the last final, so much was ending and changing. Overwhelmed by it all, she let her face fall into her hands, and she let it all out.

Chapter Nineteen

Anxious to get to the office and speak with Marissa about Isabella, Wyatt was up and out the door of his apartment bright and early. Typically, he would be excessively focused on whatever cases he was working on and would pay little to no attention to the world around him. But since meeting Isabella, he found himself walking more slowly on his way to work, taking in all that was happening around him. He had been going to the same café every morning for years and that day, for the first time ever, he made small talk with the barista who regularly made his Americano. When he got to his office building, he smiled as he walked up to the security guard on duty. He quickly checked the man's name tag before speaking. "Good morning, Jacob."

"Good morning, sir," Jacob said, swiping Wyatt's identification card while trying to not look too surprised by the sudden friendliness.

"Aren't you usually only here at night?"

"That's right, sir." Jacob nodded his head, again surprised this guy had ever noticed him. "I worked last night. You're here so early this morning that my shift is still going."

Wyatt chuckled. "Well, I hope you have a great day!"

"Thank you," Jacob looked down at the computer which scanned Wyatt's I.D. card. "Mr. Dawson."

Wyatt smiled and walked to the elevators. He had to admit to himself, letting people in and being social really put him in a good mood. Who knew?

Answering the endless emails in his inbox took a few hours that morning, and before he knew it, it was almost 10 a.m. He couldn't believe how quickly time had flown by, and now he was surprised he hadn't heard from Marissa. He picked up the phone and called her.

"Marissa, it's Wyatt, how are you this morning?"

"I'm okay, Wyatt. How are you?"

"Great, actually. But you know what would make my day even better? If you told me about that lead on finding Isabella you mentioned yesterday."

Marissa took a deep breath. She had been planning all morning how to handle the whole Ella Martinez issue, and she decided she would not tell Wyatt what she had learned. It was better if he never found out Isabella's identity. "Oh, I'm sorry, Wyatt, but that lead didn't pan out."

"Really?" Wyatt sat back in his chair.

She remained quiet.

"Okay, but you'll keep trying, right?" he asked her.

"Sure! But you know, if we don't find her, maybe that's what's meant to be?"

Wyatt nodded slowly.

"And you know, I think it's been great, the way you opened yourself up. There is a whole city out there of millions of women that would be thrilled to get to know you. Maybe now you'll start being open to meeting someone new. You know, I have a friend from business school, Delia. She's amazing, and somehow still single. Maybe I could put you two in touch?"

"No, thank you, Marissa," Wyatt said, cutting her off mid-sentence. "Thanks again for trying to help. I've got to go." He hung up the phone.

Sitting back in his chair, he swiveled around to look out the big windows at the vast city below. Of course, he understood that there were millions of women in this city, but the problem was there was only one Isabella. For some reason Marissa was giving up on the search, and to insist any more would be unprofessional on his part. That meant one thing. He was going to have to find Isabella himself.

"Mr. Dawson," Alice's voice came through his intercom. "From what I understand from Bill Kaftan's assistant, he is away in the mountains with his family for a few days."

Wyatt slumped back in his chair. "Great."

The list of intel on Isabella sat on his desk. He pulled it out and read through it again. The bookstore angle was too much of a longshot. There were too many bookstores in the city. But Isabella had also mentioned a community center that was having a play sometime soon. Determined once more, he got on his computer and searched for community centers in New York City with Christmas plays. A list of community centers popped up and Wyatt started going to each of their websites to see if they were planning Christmas plays.

The research took longer than he anticipated, and he had to stop frequently to get work done. Around 1 p.m. he had to go to a client lunch meeting which lasted much longer than it should have, but that was always the case. Once a client knew the lunch was on Dawson & Hancock, they often ordered multiple courses and even cocktails, depending on the day of the week and the time of year. On the Thursday before Christmas, the courses were being ordered in rapid fire, wine was being poured, and no one was in any rush. No one except Wyatt.

"Don't you think that's a good strategy, Wyatt?" Danielle Owens, his client, asked as she turned to him and put her hand on his arm. To everyone but Wyatt, it was clear Danielle Owens was interested in more than his opinion on her case, as she used every opportunity to touch him in some way. Everyone but Wyatt, that is.

He hadn't heard exactly what strategy Danielle was talking about, but he nodded his head anyway. "Yeah, that sounds great."

He did his best to follow the conversation and tried to push away thoughts of Isabella. That list of community centers scrolled through his mind. Some strong feeling deep down inside told him he was looking in the right place. He would find her. His phone rang and he took the opportunity to excuse himself from his clients to answer the call. "Wyatt Dawson."

"Hi Wyatt, I hope I'm not interrupting something important."

Wyatt looked toward the table where his clients drank and laughed, "Hi, Mom. No, you're not interrupting anything. How are you?"

"Oh, I'm okay. You know me and the holidays. I stress myself out and run myself ragged. It takes me weeks to recover." She laughed lightly, but they both knew this was all small talk.

"Right. How's the family?"

"Everyone's fine, dear. We miss you."

Wyatt didn't respond. His mom continued. "I know you've spoken to Alexa a few times, and she has asked about your plans for the holidays, but I thought maybe if *I* asked you, you would come home?"

Wyatt looked up at the ceiling and took a deep breath. He knew how hard it was for his mom to ask him.

"Does dad know you're calling me?"

She paused a beat, which he knew was his answer.

"Look, I know your dad is as stubborn as they come, but he misses you. I know he misses you. If you came home for the holidays, this Christmas would be different. I know it."

Before he could say no his mom quickly said, "Think about it, will you? Will you think about it before saying no? You know your dad and I, we aren't getting any younger, and..." she didn't finish the thought. There was no need to.

Wyatt sighed. "Okay, mom. I'll think about it."

Back at the table, Wyatt got through the remainder of the overly long lunch without incident. On a bitter cold day like today, Wyatt would typically hail a cab back to the office but today he needed to walk. Taking his time and looking around at all the high-end designer stores on Madison Avenue, he kept wishing he could be strolling hand in hand with Isabella. He was pretty sure she would love this area of the city, with all the shiny storefronts and window displays full of the most cutting-edge fashions. Every Christmas season his sisters, Alexa and Courtney, along with their mom, would take a trip into Manhattan to shop Madison Avenue. He remembered them returning flushed and exhausted, their hands full of shopping bags, laughing at how they "shopped til' they dropped." The memory brought him back to the conversation with his mom.

His mom wasn't one to call him much, never wanting to bother him or put him out. Every time he started to soften about the idea of going home for Christmas, he thought about the last time he was home for the holidays and the way his father had treated him. Wyatt had the big argument with his father eight years ago and didn't go back home again for Christmas for another five years. The most recent time was three years ago. Alexa and his mom had called many times, asking him to come home for Christmas just like they were doing this year. At that time, it had been so long since he'd been home that he let himself hope his father would have gotten over his career choice and be ready to make amends. Boy was he wrong.

The moment he'd walked through the front door of his childhood home, his father said, "What is *he* doing here? No one told me he was coming. Traitors are not welcome in this house. I want him out."

His mom and siblings pleaded with Wyatt to give his father another chance, but he couldn't do it. After the long drive out to Connecticut, Wyatt stayed inside the house for only a few minutes before turning around and walking out. He got in his car and made the long trip back to the city where he spent his Christmas at the office, eating takeout Chinese food and using work as a wall to protect him from the pain. Even now, as a mature adult, the memory of his father's words still stung.

As he walked down Madison Avenue, thinking about the hurt from that Christmas three years ago, he decided he wasn't going to go home this year. He couldn't put himself through that again. He didn't trust Alexa or his mom when they claimed his father had mellowed over the past few years.

The sound of a sweet Christmas carol somehow fought its way through the traffic noise on the street. When Wyatt looked up, he realized he was in front of Leighton's department store. The music he heard was coming from their Christmas-themed window display. Curiosity got the better of him and he decided he wanted to see the windows. Apparently, he wasn't the only one.; a long line of cheery people chatting and sipping hot beverages snaked down the sidewalk. He fought against the desire to walk away, and instead headed to the end of the line. Thankfully, the line moved quickly as people shuffled slowly past the window, gawking at the details.

While he crept along, he checked emails on his phone, and before long he was standing at the window. He was immediately glad he had waited. The display was alive with snow activities! Faux snow blanketed the scene and fell gently from the "sky" in a continuous sprinkle. In the center of the display there was a gigantic mountain with little skiers gliding down its face, and a chair lift bringing others to the top. Little smiling figurines were sledding down a hill, their faces appearing to be in mid-laugh. A cheery ice-skating rink was filled with little figures twirling in brightly colored skirts.

Wyatt took his time—he didn't want to miss a thing. Off to the side there was an epic snowball fight happening, and there was even a dogsled race going on, too. Sprinkled throughout the scene were snow-shoers and cross-country skiers, and babies being pulled in sleds. The music was like rock n' roll meets Christmastime and it was impossible not to smile at it all. He wanted to jump right into that display and have some winter fun. Whew—now that was a mood swing!

Once he was all the way past the window, he was consumed with a Christmas spirit he hadn't felt since he was eight years old. Still smiling, he pulled open Leighton's front doors. He was going to go Christmas shopping.

Leaving behind the ruckus and chaos that is a New York City sidewalk at Christmastime, Wyatt pushed through Leighton's massive double doors. It felt like he had stepped into a different world. The Christmas music playing throughout the store was a soft

146

instrumental piece, the lighting was bright, and somehow, despite all the shoppers, it was peaceful. A woman with stiff hair and too much makeup approached him. Her smile was unnaturally white, and her eyelashes were so long they reminded him of a Venus Flytrap plant.

"Hello there! My name's Lisa." She smiled and batted her eyelashes. "Can I help you with your shopping today?"

Out of habit Wyatt was about to turn her down, but something made him change his mind. "I would love some help, Lisa!"

Her face lit up with surprise. "Wonderful! What, or who, are you shopping for? Someone special in your life?" She batted those long lashes again.

"There, is actually," he said, letting her down easy. "But I'm not shopping for her right now. Today I need gifts for my mother, two sisters, and my niece." He figured he would start with all the females first, since they seemed much harder to buy for.

"Oh, wow! We have our work cut out for us, don't we? But no worries, you lucked out. I'm the best shopper here. Let's start with your mom."

After asking questions about the likes and dislikes of his family members, along with their ages and coloring (Wyatt had no idea why she wanted to know if Alexa was a blonde or a brunette and what color eyes she had), Lisa led him around the store and gave him options. It took quite a bit of time, but still he found himself enjoying being part of the gift-buying process. In the past, he had always asked Alice or Marissa to pick out, buy, and ship the gifts for his family. But today he picked out a silk scarf for his mother, perfume for Alexa, a handbag for Courtney (which Lisa called a "clutch"), and a gold pendant necklace with the initial *K* for his niece Kayla. Shopping for his family gave him the opportunity to appreciate them. He felt like it brought him closer to his family members. As he described Kayla's long honey-colored hair and green eyes, he suddenly felt a longing to see her. In fact, he missed them all, maybe even his dad.

As he waited for Lisa to wrap all the gifts, he walked to the café that was attached to the store and bought himself the seasonal special, some type of mocha something-or-other. He usually took his coffee black, and this drink, although delicious, felt like eating a dessert. He hated to admit it, but he was starting to understand why people enjoyed Christmas shopping.

While he sat in the café drinking his mocha-thingy, a woman stepped up to the counter to order a drink. She was older, maybe in her sixties. As she laughed and chatted with the barista, it became clear they knew each other well. He noticed the woman wore a Leighton's staff badge, and he heard the barista ask her, "Would you like the regular?" to which she nodded.

The woman was petite, with olive skin and dark hair. Nothing about this woman struck him as out of the ordinary, until he heard her name. The barista had finished making her drink and called out, "Regina! It's ready!"

Wyatt's ears perked up when he heard the name *Regina*. He shifted his eyes away from his phone. The woman, perhaps sensing Wyatt was looking at her, smiled warmly at him. He smiled back and said, "Merry Christmas."

She smiled and said the same.

Regina was not a common name. Marissa had told him how a woman named Regina had come to their office to pick up a coat that was accidentally left behind at the party. Marissa had been sure Regina had some connection to Isabella, but she said once she investigated it further, she was wrong. What if she wasn't wrong? What if Regina knew Isabella? Could this be the same Regina? He did remember Marissa mentioning something about the woman being on the older side.

At the risking of looking like a complete crazy person, Wyatt stood up and started toward the café door Regina had exited. Once in the department store, he scanned the area, which was a maze of makeup and jewelry counters and packed full of shoppers. He looked all around for the petite, older woman. She had only been a few steps ahead of him, how far could she have gone? It was as if she had disappeared. He walked quickly to the double front doors to see if perhaps she was outside, but he couldn't see her anywhere amongst the crowd out on the sidewalk. Turning back around, he made one last scan of the store and…nothing.

This Regina woman clearly worked for Leighton's, maybe one of the employees knew her. Driven by this new hope, Wyatt walked up to the first employee he saw, a woman working behind a makeup counter. "Excuse me."

She smiled up at him, ready to make a sale. "How can I help you?"

"I am looking for a woman who works here, her name is Regina. Do you know where I might be able to find her?"

The woman frowned and shook her head. "I'm sorry. There are hundreds of people that work here, especially during the holidays. Hundreds of them. Unless she works right here in the makeup or fragrance department, I wouldn't know her."

Wyatt's shoulders sagged. He thanked the makeup woman for her time and made his way back over to Lisa in the gift-wrapping area. There was no way to know what department Regina worked in, and it would take him hours to go through all five floors of the store, asking for her in every single department. He suddenly felt silly. Even if this Regina was connected to Ella, which was a longshot, what did that even signify? The whole Regina search was an echo of his desire to find Isabella.

Lisa was finished wrapping the gifts and had put them in shopping bags for Wyatt. He thanked her profusely for her help and wished her a Merry Christmas. It felt good to have the gifts purchased and checked off his mental to-do list. Of course, that made him think of his nephew Michael, and the almost-impossible autographed basketball request. He really didn't want to let his nephew, or his sister, down. Wouldn't it be great to give Michael the basketball in person and see his reaction?

Chapter Twenty

The moment Ella walked through the front door of the Manhattan Community Center, she was bombarded with music, laughter and commotion. The auditorium was a beehive of activity and Ella felt her spirits rise. Bonnie, who must have arrived sometime while Ella was gone, came running up to her.

"Ella! This is unbelievable! I don't know how you pulled this off or how I can ever repay you for this. But thank you!" Her light blue eyes were shiny. She grabbed Ella in a giant hug, squeezing her so tight that she had trouble breathing.

"Don't thank me yet. There's still a lot of work to do." She pointed toward the stage. "Let's go see how things are coming along."

Up on the stage, Ella stopped dead in her tracks when her eyes found Liana Lapierre. The queen of style was sitting on the floor, barefoot, sewing feathers onto some type of headpiece.

"Ms. Lapierre, I'm sorry! Let me find you a chair!"

Liana laughed. "No, no, no. I don't mind at all." She waved Ella off. "When I first started out many years ago, I had one chair in my studio. Once I added a couple staff members, we would share the chair, constantly taking turns. Why we didn't just buy another chair?" Liana shrugged.

"I'll tell you why!" Marney jumped into the conversation. "Because you were too cheap!" The two old friends laughed loudly.

"I wasn't cheap, Marney. I was thrifty! Spend a few hundred dollars on a new chair or buy more fabric to work with—the choice was easy for me."

"Oh, those were the days," Marney said wistfully, her eyes glazing over at the memories.

"Yes, they were." Liana smiled. "Now everyone who works for me gets a chair! See how far we've come!" They laughed again.

Liana turned to Ella. "But seriously, sitting here today on the floor, creating wild and vibrant costumes for children, all sewed by hand...I can't remember a time when I felt this happy. This has brought me back to my one true love—art. I love creating art. And somewhere along the line, I lost that. The expectations and pressures for me to succeed year after year...I became like a robot."

Ella and Marney nodded in understanding as Liana continued. "I want to thank you, Ella. And you too, Marney. This," she spread her arms out, motioning to the giant pile of half-finished costumes, "This has been a gift. A gift I didn't even know I needed."

"Okay, that's enough sappy stuff, Li," Marney said. "Let's all get back to work." She turned to Bonnie and asked, "What time are the children arriving for dress rehearsal?"

"The kids should be arriving at 4 o'clock for dress rehearsal, and opening curtain is at seven."

Ella looked at her phone. "That means we have three more hours to get all the costumes finished before everyone gets here. We'll have to be sure to allow some time to make any fit adjustments."

"Back to work!" Marney yelled.

Despite the looming dress rehearsal deadline, the mood among all those volunteering was not frantic or panicked. It was a fun project, especially for creative people. Ella marveled at the finished products and was bursting with anticipation for the kids to see their new costumes. Marney and Liana sat near each other, sewing away while telling old stories. Every member of the glam squad inched their way closer and closer to Liana and Marney, straining their ears, and even turning down the Christmas music to hear the stories from Liana Lapierre's early days.

Every now and then, especially after a really good tale, they would whisper among themselves, finding it hard to reconcile the Liana Lapierre who was a strict boss with impossible expectations of her crew, with the young, driven "Li" who worked until 11 p.m. and then went out dancing until 3:00 in the morning. This was a side of Liana they thought they would never see…they didn't even know it existed! And they were enthralled.

The volunteers were having such a good time, comfortably lost in their work and time seemed to fly by. Right around 4 o'clock, kids started to trickle in, along with other Center volunteers who were helping with the play. The auditorium erupted in chatter, laughter, and squeals of joy as the children were surprised by their new costumes. There were lots of jaws dropping and eyes widening, and lots and lots of "thank yous" and hugs. It was a beautiful sight.

Once all the costumes had been tried on and nipped here and tucked there, the kids helped clean up the mess. There was fabric on every surface, including Bob Cratchit's desk and chair. And sequins were positively *everywhere!* Supplies were gathered up and thrown back into suitcases. Small pieces of cotton and silk were tossed in large bags to be repurposed for another project.

Once the stage and backstage were finally cleaned up, the kids bustled around the center with nervous energy, ready to go over the play one time before curtain call at seven. Small groups were gathered here and there rehearsing their scenes. The director, Sam Stafford, patiently began the last run-through of the play. He was a famed Broadway director, who volunteered his time with the Center every Christmas season.

Growing up in Harlem with few opportunities available to him in the arts, in his early teens he started taking the bus down to the theater district and sneaking into shows. It was like his world came alive as he marveled at the scenery, the costumes, the music, the *talent!* From that point forward, he knew what he wanted to do, and he went after it with laser-like focus.

Being able to introduce kids at the Manhattan Community Center to the theater was a blessing and it filled his heart with joy.

Although it might sound cliché, he got way more out of it than they did. Tonight's performance held more weight than any previous show he had helped with. The center was losing its funding and once the kids found out, they would be devastated. This show had to be spectacular, not only so that the center could go out with a *bang!* But also, as a last-ditch effort to drum up some support and funding for the center, he had invited some theater industry folks to the show. He kept this information to himself, however, to avoid any chance of disappointment.

He ran through the show with the kids, prompting them on their lines, reminding them where to stand, and to speak louder. His stomach was a knot of nerves. He could help a little, but what the center needed was too much for him alone to provide. He needed to help keep this place open!

Chapter Twenty-One

After the long client lunch, the phone call from his mother, and the shopping spree at Leighton's, Wyatt was grateful to be alone in his quiet office. He'd enjoyed the window display and the Christmas shopping, but when he thought about the autographed basketball, he started to feel overwhelmed. The expectations of people this time of year were too high for any mortal human being to meet. It was all a set up for disappointment. Clients expected a party at every meeting. Everyone wanted gifts. People expected you to become a totally different person. No one from his family bothered him all year long, but here in the middle of December, suddenly everyone missed him and thought he should come visit.

Wyatt moved his mouse to turn on his computer, and the list of community centers was still open on the screen. He had already looked at websites and made notes on the list, now it was time for real action. He picked up the phone and started calling each center on the list, asking if an Isabella volunteered there. After about an hour of phone calls, he called the Manhattan Community Center up in Harlem.

A young man answered the phone. "Manhattan Community Center," he said in a rushed voice.

"Hi, yes. I was wondering if someone named Isabella volunteers there?"

"Ummmm, not sure. We have an Ella that volunteers here— is that who you mean?"

Ella. "I'm not sure. Are you putting on a Christmas play this holiday season?"

"Yeah! That's why I'm kinda in a rush, ya know? It's tonight. Starts in a few."

"The play is tonight? What time?"

"Curtain goes up at seven. So, if that's all you need… "

"Right, of course. Thank you."

Could Isabella be Ella? There was only one way to find out. Wyatt looked at the clock. It was six-thirty. He had barely enough time to get to the Manhattan Community Center for the start of the play.

Chapter Twenty-Two

A few minutes before seven, the actors and actresses scurried backstage. The curtain was drawn, and adult volunteers went around hushing everyone. Every now and then a kid would peek out from the side of the curtain to look at the gathering crowd. Ella kept telling them not to look, that it would only make them all more nervous, but they couldn't help themselves. *If you can't beat 'em, join 'em,* Ella thought, and she, too, peeked out at the crowd. There *were way* more people in the audience than she expected to see, and even more people were streaming in as the start of the play grew nearer.

Backstage, the children's nerves and excitement were palpable. The air buzzed with expectation and anxiety. The adult volunteers smiled, doing their best to appear calm. They adjusted costumes and offered words of encouragement. Finally, it was time. Sam gave one short but powerful pep talk, and everyone took their places. Ella waited on the side of the stage, behind a curtain where she couldn't be seen by the audience. It was her job to send the children onto the stage when it was their turn to perform.

The play started off without a hitch. Actually, there were quite a few hitches, but that made it all the more heartwarming. The children were adorable, each one taking their part seriously. The audience laughed when they were supposed to laugh, and "awwwed" when they were supposed to "aww."

During the intermission, Ella congratulated those who had performed already, and prepared the next group of performers for the stage. When satisfied everyone was ready for the second half, she once again took her position behind the curtain. She looked out at the audience, hoping to make eye contact with Marney, Liana, or one of the members of the glam squad. As her eyes scanned the crowd, they fell on a tall, dark, handsome man in a suit who was standing at the end of an aisle. Ella sucked in her breath, unable to breathe. Wyatt Dawson. Here.

The room spun around her and she felt like she might faint. Joana, who stood nearby wearing her Ghost of Christmas Future costume, noticed the color drain from Ella's face.

"Miss Ella, is something wrong? Are you okay?"

"I...I...I'm fine," Ella stammered.

"You look like you saw a ghost!" Joana giggled at her own joke, but she got no laugh out of Ella. "Get it?" she continued. "Because I'm dressed like a ghost?"

Ella managed a smile. She took a few deep breaths, trying to pull herself together. Slowly, she peeked out at the audience again to be sure her eyes weren't playing tricks on her. Wyatt Dawson at a community center's Christmas play in Harlem? What were the odds of that being a coincidence?

"Who are you lookin' at?" Joana followed Ella's gaze.

Ella quickly pulled herself back. "Nothing. No one. It was...no one."

Joana eyed her suspiciously. "Do you have a boyfriend out there? 'Cause the only time I see girls act like you're acting, all sweaty and can't catch their breath, is 'cause of a boy."

Ella laughed nervously. "No, Joana. I don't have a...he's not a boyfriend." She took a deep breath. "Okay, Joana, this is your big scene. Are you ready?"

"Oh yeah, I'm ready. I'm going to break a leg!" Ella laughed.

At that moment Marney came running up to her, breathless. "Oh, my goodness! Oh, my goodness! Ella, you are not going to believe who is in the audience!"

"I know," Ella groaned.

Marney pulled back, skeptical. "No, I don't think you know."

"Yes, I do, Marney. And I'm trying not to think about it."

"This could be the big break the community center has been looking for! He might be willing to become a sponsor! To donate to save the center!"

Ella scrunched up her face, confused. "Wait, who are you talking about?"

"Benjamin Scott!"

"Who is Benjamin Scott?"

"You don't know who Benjamin Scott is? He's only one of the biggest of the big- wigs on the Broadway scene. He invests in plays, he produces, he writes, he directs..."

Ella was nodding her head, understanding now why Marney was excited. "Wow, that *is* great news! How did he hear about the play?"

"I guess Sam Stafford called in some favors. He asked some of his friends in the business to come support the center."

"That's amazing! And very generous of Sam! Oh my gosh— fingers crossed that someone falls in love with this place and wants to help! I mean, look at that face," she pointed at Joana who was dramatically rehearsing her lines. "How can you not fall in love with that face?"

Marney smiled, watching Joana. "Wait a minute, who did *you* think I was talking about?"

Ella busied herself with the microphone headpiece she had on. The volunteers were all wearing them so they could communicate with each other. Ella was suddenly very interested in hers and kept checking and re-checking to make sure it was working.

"Isabella Martinez, you look at me right now and tell me who is in that audience."

Ella sighed. There was no way Marney was going to let this go. "Wyatt Dawson."

Marney's hazel eyes widened, and she put her hand to her heart, like she was about to recite the Pledge of Allegiance. "Wyatt Dawson is here?"

Ella nodded.

"You know what this means, don't you?"

Here it comes, Ella thought.

"This, my dear Isabella, this is fate! He must have come here looking for you! Did you tell him you volunteered at this community center?"

"No," Ella admitted, shaking her head. She thought back to her conversation with Wyatt the night of the party. "I may have told him I volunteered at *a* community center, but I definitely didn't mention which one."

"He must have searched until he found the right one!" Marney was bursting with excitement, her eyes dancing under the twinkle lights that lined the hallway from the stage to the backstage.

"Marney," Ella placed her hands on her friend's bouncing shoulders. This was a common occurrence in their friendship, and it was Ella's way of bringing Marney back down to earth when she got carried away. "There must be hundreds of community centers throughout the city. I doubt 'New York City's most eligible bachelor' took the time to search out which one I volunteer at."

"I think you're wrong, my dear!"

"This isn't one of those sappy romance novels you like to read. This is real life. I am Isabella Martinez, and things like that don't happen to me."

Marney held out her hand.

"What? What are you doing?"

"Hand over your headset. I will man the stage; you go out and say hello to him."

Ella shook her head frantically from side to side, "Have you lost your mind? I cannot go talk to him! He doesn't know the real me! He probably wouldn't even recognize me! He thinks I'm glamorous Isabella, not plain ol' Ella."

"Ella, you are anything but plain. Even with your hair back and no makeup on, your beauty shines through. This is your chance! Wyatt Dawson is only a few yards away! You have got to say hello."

"Two minutes until curtain!" one of the stage crew volunteers yelled throughout the backstage.

"Marney, go back and watch the play. I've got to make sure it runs smoothly, especially with that guy, that Benjamin Smart in the audience."

Marney rolled her eyes. "It's Benjamin Scott."

"Right. He's here and that is more important."

Marney shook her head in disappointment and walked slowly back to her seat in the audience.

Watching the older woman walk away, Ella's heart hurt knowing she had disappointed her. But she wasn't ready for Wyatt to know her identity. Maybe she never would be.

"Okay, Ghost of Christmas Future, are you ready for your stage debut?" She smiled at Joana.

"Ready as I'll ever be!"

#

Thankfully the children were unaware of the significance of the play. They delivered their lines with gusto and sometimes giggles. When it was over the audience was on their feet, cheering. After bowing to the crowd, Sam called the entire cast and crew up on stage for a group bow. The crowd's cheering grew even louder. Ella's heart soared and her eyes filled with tears when she saw the look of pride on the faces of the children.

The applause finally died down and Sam thanked everyone for their support. He thanked the children and the spectators, as well as Bonnie and her entire staff. He then called out for all the volunteers to come out onto the stage. Ella froze where she stood. Other volunteers were shuffling past her to get to the stage nudging her out of the way. What should she do? She couldn't go out there—Wyatt would see her!

Chapter Twenty-Three

Wyatt arrived at the Manhattan Community Center a little after seven o'clock. He ran in, knowing he was late, and gave the young man selling tickets double the ticket price as a donation. The man thanked him repeatedly. Wyatt nodded quickly and rushed to the auditorium, following the signs that had been hung throughout the center. He was surprised by the amount of people packed into the space. Every seat was taken and there were people standing in the back and at the ends of the aisles. His heart thumped in his chest at the thought of seeing Isabella again. Would she really be here? It was hard to believe that after searching for her for days, he would finally get to see her.

He quickly assessed the layout of the room and decided to stand in the back corner, where he had a decent view of the stage but wasn't being crowded by other spectators. The play had already begun. Although anxious for the play to be over with, once he started paying attention to the production, he really enjoyed it. It had been a long time since Wyatt had watched any type of Christmas show, whether that be a play or a movie. His sisters were always getting together to watch Hallmark Christmas movies, but he had never indulged.

When it became obvious that one of the kids was struggling to remember his lines, Wyatt wished he could help. One boy tried to subtly look backstage, where someone must have fed him the line, because suddenly he smiled and delivered it perfectly. The kids

were so earnest and sweet that Wyatt was found himself routing for
them

During intermission he continually scanned the room for
signs of Isabella. Then a jarring thought occurred to him—would he
recognize her? He thought back to the night of the Christmas party
and pictured her shy smile and large brown eyes. He would
recognize her. Intermission came and went, and there was no sign
of her. Was she there? What if he'd gotten bad information from the
young man that had answered the phone earlier? Wyatt could be at
the wrong place. What if Isabella isn't the Ella that volunteered
here? He cursed himself for not having asked more questions, like
what does Ella look like? He didn't even know how old the Ella that
volunteered here was. He should have at least asked that! Or, does
Ella also work at a bookstore? Is she a student at NYU? These
would all have been great questions to ask before braving the rush-
hour traffic to get all the way up to Harlem.

When the show was over, Wyatt was surprised when the
director got up on stage to thank everyone, and it turned out to be
Sam Stafford. Wyatt had met Sam a few years ago at an event for a
show Sam was producing. He was impressed the center had
convinced Sam to direct since he was such a big player in the
Broadway world. Wyatt made a mental note to say hello afterward.

Sam called up all the children and they took another bow.
Everyone was beaming with pride. He then called a woman named
Bonnie up to the stage. She apparently ran the center. Sam thanked
the audience members next, and Wyatt could feel his heart rate start
to quicken. Isabella should be called to the stage soon, too. As he
thought this, Sam asked all the center volunteers to come out on
stage and be recognized for their support.

The volunteers began trickling onto the stage, all wearing
Manhattan Community Center logo polo shirts. Wyatt searched
their faces, straining to see if one of the women was Isabella. The
stream of volunteers eventually stopped, and no one else emerged
from backstage. Everyone was now on the stage and Isabella was
not there. Disappointment hit Wyatt like a snowball to the gut.

Deep down he thought this was the community center where Isabella helped. Did he get it completely wrong?

Unwilling to give up completely, he waited until most of the crowd had filed out. He spotted Sam talking to an older woman, and he approached them. Sam saw Wyatt, and his face broke into a smile.

"Wyatt Dawson. What a surprise! What brings you here?" The two shook hands.

"I know, it's been too long, Sam. How are you?"

"I'm good!" He turned to the woman by his side. "This is Marney Winters, an old friend of mine."

Wyatt extended his hand, and she did the same. "It's a pleasure to meet you Ms. Winters."

"Oh, my. Call me Marney, please!" Marney shook Wyatt's hand rapidly. She seemed to be bursting with energy and light, and her eyes were warm and friendly. Wyatt liked her immediately. "It's strange," she continued coyly, "I feel as though we've met before. Is it possible I've seen you somewhere else?"

Sam started laughing, "I know where you've seen him. Marney, you won't believe this, but you're talking to 'New York City's Most Eligible Bachelor!'"

Wyatt's cheeks turned red as a Santa suit. "Please, don't hold it against me, Marney."

She giggled. "Wow! Who knew I'd be in the presence of New York City royalty! How do you two know each other?" She pointed back and forth between the two men.

"We met a few years ago at a publicity event for *LadyBird*, a show Sam was producing."

Sam nodded. "That seems like ages ago! And Wyatt here was invited, not only because he's a good-looking, successful bachelor, but because he represented one of the other investors in the show who was being sued for something bogus. He's darn good at his job. Mike Dern will forever be grateful."

"You volunteer your time here with the kids?" Wyatt asked Sam, uncomfortable with the flattery.

"I do. I grew up in the neighborhood and I have been helping with their Christmas play for years now. It's an amazing place, these kids are something else."

"I was really impressed by the play; you should be proud."

A woman in a fitted black blazer and skirt walked over to the group. She buzzed with an energy that demanded attention, and all eyes were on her.

Marney smiled. "Sam, Wyatt, this is Liana Lapierre, the fashion designer, and one of my oldest friends." Everyone shook hands and said hello. "Who knew this event would attract so many VIP's," Marney giggled. "Sam is a famous Broadway director, and Wyatt is a big-time attorney. And let's not forget, he's also—"

"Please don't say it," Wyatt interrupted.

"I'll leave that part out," Marney winked. But even if she had introduced him as an alien from Mars, Liana and Sam would not have noticed. The two had locked eyes the moment they met and had already started their own side conversation. Marney and Wyatt smiled at each other, knowingly.

"I must be going now, Wyatt, but I must say it has been an absolute pleasure meeting you," Marney said as she extended her hand once more.

"The pleasure is all mine, I assure you." Wyatt smiled.

Before they parted, an idea popped into Marney's mind. "Wait, you're an attorney? Now that I think of it..." she hesitated, pretending to be unsure. Wyatt nodded in response. "I may be in need of your services."

"Really? I hope everything's okay."

"I'm not sure. Do you think you could come see me at my store tomorrow? Do you do that? Go to your client versus them coming to you?"

"For you, Marney, of course. Where is your store?"

Digging in her giant handbag that was stuffed with receipts, snacks, makeup and who knew what else, she fished out a business card and handed it to Wyatt. "This is me! The store opens at ten and I'll be there all day until closing."

After another proper good-bye to Wyatt, Sam, and Liana, Marney left. Looking around one more time to be sure he hadn't somehow missed Isabella, Wyatt sighed and realized it was time for him to leave as well. With the promise to "grab lunch" with Sam soon, he started to walk toward the door. His heart felt heavy. He had been sure this was the right community center. Before he put on his overcoat, he reached into his pocket for his phone, and found the business card Marney had given him. When he read the name of the store, he stopped mid-stride. The Book Nook. A smile was fixed to his face as he got into his awaiting car. *It had to be the one.*

Chapter Twenty-Four

The play was a huge success. The costumes had dazzled the audience and the children were beaming with pride and joy. Ella should be proud and happy too, but instead she found it hard to even fake a smile. As she helped clean up the backstage area, her heart twisted inside her chest. With every breath she struggled to hold back her tears. By the end of the night, in the quiet, empty auditorium, her entire body ached with exhaustion.

Ella watched Liana Lapierre and Sam Stafford leave together to have a late dinner. She was happy for them, but it also made her feel that much lonelier.

Bonnie was overflowing with gratitude and hope, as she was sure the success of the play would bring them a new sponsor. She would be praying for that Christmas miracle. Ella hugged Bonnie, sending her own prayers to her, but tears sprung to her eyes when she realized she no longer believed in the idea of miracles.

It was late when she got home to her modest little apartment in Queens. Not wanting to wake her mother, she quietly tip-toed through the kitchen.

"Ella, honey. Is that you?"

"Mom?" Her mom never waited up for her. "Are you okay?"

Her mom chuckled. "Of course, I'm okay! I wanted to hear all about the Christmas play! I'm sorry I couldn't be there, the store is crazy right now, and they needed me to stay later than usual," she said with a sigh.

"I understand, Mom. There's no need to explain." She smiled at Regina while taking off her coat. She plunked down in the faded, comfy chair in the living room. Her mom was curled up on the couch; a soft blanket was wrapped around her shoulders. A Christmas romance novel rested on her lap and a cup of steaming tea sat on the side table.

"How was it?" she asked excitedly.

"The play? Oh, the play was great—better than great. The place was packed with people. We got the costumes made in time, and the kids were adorable. It was a huge success by all measures." Ella smiled, but it didn't reach her eyes.

"That's wonderful, hon!" Her mom looked at her closely. "If the play went so well, then why do you look on the verge of tears? Did something happen?"

When Ella was much younger, she had always been able to hold in her tears. If there was a problem at school with a schoolmate or a teacher, she would lock down her feelings and not let anyone see she was upset. Even once she got home, she would hold it together. However, as soon as she talked to her mom or dad about whatever was bothering her, the floodgates would open. The moment they would ask her what was wrong—because of course they always knew when something was wrong—she would burst into tears.

Apparently, the same thing still happened today. When Regina asked her if she was okay, tears began to slide down her cheeks like two little streams. Regina closed her book and put it on the end table. She opened her arms wide, reaching out to her daughter. Like she did when she was a little girl, she slid into her mom's embrace and let it all out.

Ella launched into a long, detailed account of everything that had happened since the night of the Christmas party.

Regina was always an excellent listener and did her best not to react to any of the information that Ella bombarded her with. This was easier said than done, especially when Ella told her about her final exam performance. She was shocked—it was out of character for her daughter to be irresponsible about her schoolwork. Meeting Wyatt Dawson had clearly turned Ella's life upside down.

Once Ella had told her mom everything, she looked over at her, curious for her response. Regina took a few moments to gather her thoughts and then finally spoke. "Isabella, you have always been driven. And once your father passed away, you became even more so. I always thanked God for sending you to me. You were disciplined, determined and ambitious and I thought I would never have to worry about you. But as you have gotten older, I *have* worried about you. I've worried that you don't take time to enjoy your life. You don't hold anyone close to your heart—not even friends or love interests." She paused to let that last sentence sink in. A fresh set of tears slipped down Ella's cheeks.

"I don't say this to upset you. This comes from my heart," Regina said softly, touching Ella's arm. Ella nodded. "It seems to me that while you were dressed up you felt like a totally different person, and you were able to open up your heart and let someone in. It also seems that the experience threw your entire life out of balance. And balance is the key. Of course, it's important to work hard and study hard, and I'm proud of you for that. But life is not worth living if you don't have people to share it with."

"You're right, Mom. Thank you." Ella mopped up her face with a tissue. "But what do I do now?"

Regina thought for a moment. "What was dad's favorite saying?"

"*Nunca dejes de soñar.*"

Regina nodded. "What are you dreaming of right now, honey?"

Ella didn't even need to think before answering. "Wyatt." Just saying his name made her smile.

"Okay, then what are you going to do about it?" Her mother challenged her.

"But what if he is expecting glamorous Isabella?"

Regina held her daughter's face in her hands as she spoke. "You *are* glamorous Isabella. That was you."

Tears sprung to Ella's eyes once again, but this time they were grateful tears full of hope and joy. She wasn't quite sure she was back to believing in Christmas miracles, but she *was* sure she was going to make her own dreams come true.

The next morning, Ella woke up full of nervous excitement. It was Friday. Almost a week had gone by since the Dawson & Hancock Christmas party, and it was only two days before Christmas. A lot was going to happen today, and she was brimming with nervous anticipation.

Today she would find out her grades for what was supposed to be her final semester of college. She had to work at The Book Nook, and she also had to clean Wyatt's offices tonight. And sometime during the day, she planned to reach out to Wyatt. She wasn't exactly sure how she was going to do that, but she had a feeling Marney would be helpful with that task.

She put on her favorite pair of jeans and her only cashmere sweater, which happened to be red, and she was feeling confident. Perhaps she should wear clothes that made her feel good all the time? The thought made her laugh, because the answer was obvious. Why had it taken her this long to realize that?

She wore tall leather boots and finished off the look with gold dangly earrings and a gold cuff bracelet. Her bare neck was a painful reminder of the missing pendant necklace, but she didn't dwell on it. As she was about to pull her hair up into her daily bun, she changed her mind and left it down. Using a curling iron on the ends, she created a gentle wave. After brushing on a little blush, mascara and lip gloss, Ella stared at her reflection in the mirror. It was as if she had created the perfect balance between Isabella and Ella. It felt right.

With a skip in her step, she walked to the subway station platform. Victor, the vendor at her usual bodega, yelled out to her that she looked nice. She smiled and stopped to buy a coffee and today's *New York Post*. There was a window seat available on the train—this was her day! Making herself comfortable, she balanced the coffee between her legs and then opened the newspaper. Staring right back at her, in black and white print, was a photo of Wyatt

Dawson. She smiled, until she realized he was with a pretty blonde. Ella's heart stopped. She scanned the article:

> ### *New York City's Most Eligible Bachelor Update!*
> *Wyatt Dawson, founder and partner at Dawson & Hancock, Esq., may not be so eligible anymore! Last week we saw him dance the night away with a beautiful brunette, and this week here he is dining with a blonde. Will a redhead be next or is this blonde the one? Anyone feeling like they want to try being a redhead for the holidays? I know I am...*

Ella read the article twice. Her hope and excitement from earlier melted away like icicles in the midday sun. A drip at a time, her dreams slipped from her body and splashed on the subway train floor. Doubt and despair filled the space in her heart that love had just vacated. *What was I thinking? Wyatt Dawson, in love with me? I must have lost my mind.* She sat in a stunned silence for the remainder of the train ride, staring out the window but seeing only her thoughts.

"Why, don't you look lovely today, Ella!" Marney smiled warmly when Ella entered The Book Nook.

"Thank you, Marney. Honestly, I don't know why I bothered."

"What do you mean? What happened?

Ella marched over to where Marney stood behind the register and slapped the newspaper down in front of her. *"This* is what happened."

Marney looked at the paper and read the article quickly. "You don't know if this is true! It doesn't say these two are dating. It doesn't even say the woman's name anywhere."

"It didn't say my name either, when they put the photo of me in the paper."

"I don't believe it," Marney scoffed, throwing the paper in the garbage can. "I saw him last night at the community center, and he was looking for *you*. He was there for you, Isabella!"

Ella shrugged. She desperately wanted to believe Marney, but this rollercoaster of emotions was too much for her to take. The bell chimed again, and they both turned around to see who it was. A tall man with dark hair stepped into the store, his back to them as he closed the door.

It couldn't be, could it? Right now, while they're talking about him? Could it be Wyatt? Marney thought to herself. As the man took off his winter hat, her hopes were squashed. It wasn't him.

"Hi there, welcome to The Book Nook," Ella said, smiling at the man. "Can I help you find something?"

One look at Ella and the man suddenly became very friendly...and very interested in books. For the opportunity to spend time with her, he started asking question after question. Marney watched from afar, wanting to give the man the stink-eye, but he was also a customer. What a predicament she found herself in. *Wyatt better get in touch soon or he may lose his chance!*

"Ella, could I see you over here for a minute?" She politely interrupted Ella and the handsome customer.

"Of course," she answered. "Would you mind excusing me for a minute?" she asked the man, who smiled at her and watched her walk away.

"What is it?" Ella asked Marney when they were standing next to each other by the register.

"Oh, it's...well, I thought..." Marney wracked her brain for an excuse for pulling Ella away from the customer. "Your grades! Don't your grades come out today?"

"They do! I completely forgot. I'm afraid to look." Ella's face twisted with concern.

"I'm sure it'll be fine. I'll go finish helping that man," Marney said disdainfully. "You should go use the computer in the back room."

Ella nodded. Her stomach was now a bundle of nerves. Marney smiled widely as she walked toward the man. Once he saw

Marney would be the one helping him, he grabbed the first book he saw and told her he was ready to check out. That was easy.

In the back room, Ella sat down at the big old computer. As she waited for the screen to come to life, she closed her eyes and took a deep breath. In all the chaos of the last week, she had forgotten what a big moment this was. This moment had been six long hard years in the making. If she passed all her classes this semester, she would officially have her bachelor's degree in Early Education. It would be the start of the future she had been planning since high school. She would become a New York State teacher. Her nights would be spent grading papers and creating lesson plans instead of cleaning bathrooms. She would no longer have to work two jobs to pay for college classes. And although she couldn't imagine not seeing Marney every day, she would stop working at The Book Nook.

Ella's foot tapped the floor impatiently as she logged into the university's student portal. She held her breath and clicked on her name, waiting for her grades to load onto the screen. She scanned the report and a scream escaped her mouth, which she quickly covered with her hand.

Marney came rushing to the back room. "What? What is it? What happened?"

Ella jumped up and turned around. "I did it! I passed!" She leapt over to Marney and they hugged, bouncing up and down together.

"I knew you could do it!" Marney laughed, hugging her tightly.

"Oh, Marney, I can't believe it! Finally, something has gone right! I need to call my mom!" Marney smiled as she watched her. She was excited for her good friend.

"I can't believe I'm going to be a teacher! I no longer need to work two jobs!" A thought occurred to Ella and her smile faded. "Oh Marney, what am I going to do without you?"

"Don't worry about me! You have your whole life to get on with! I am over-joyed and excited for you, my Isabella," Marney's eyes filled with tears.

"I'll come visit you all the time, I promise! And I'll make sure you find someone great to replace me here at the store. I won't leave until we've found the perfect person."

"Please, don't worry about it. Go call your mom!"

Ella gave Marney one last hug and picked up her phone to call her mom. To give her privacy, Marney walked to the front of the store. Her heart was bursting with conflicted feelings. Of course, she was proud and excited for Ella, who was moving on with her life and going after her dreams. But sadness needled its way inside as she thought of how lonely the store would be without her. Swiftly wiping her eyes so Ella wouldn't see the tears, she found some books to put away. It was better to keep busy.

Chapter Twenty-Five

Wyatt surprised himself by whistling as he walked the wild streets of New York City on his way into the office. Today was the day he would get to see Isabella in person once again, and the thought had him feeling so light he was sure he could float away. In the lobby he grabbed a newspaper, said a quick hello to the security guard, and made his way to the elevators. His phone rang. He looked down and saw it was Alexa.

"Good morning, Alexa. You're up early."

"Good morning! You're not the only Dawson who works in this family, Wyatt. We work hard here at Dawson Sporting Goods."

Had she been anyone else, Wyatt would have feared he had insulted her but with Alexa, he knew she let most things roll off her back. This was the reason she was the Manager of Client Relations at the family company. "Of course, you do. I didn't mean to imply otherwise."

"I'm calling to check in. How are things looking for the Damian Hawk autographed basketball?"

"Alexa," Wyatt sighed. "You only asked me yesterday. This is not an easy request! In fact, it's an almost impossible request."

"I know, I'm sorry. But it's all I can think about. Michael has a poster of Damian Hawk hanging in his room and every time I go in, I think about it."

"I reached out to Bill Kaftan, but he's away for the holidays with his family. I don't know any other avenue to get to Hawk. I think you need to start thinking about a plan B."

"Okay, I will," Alexa said. Wyatt could hear the disappointment in her voice. "Do you know anyone else who knows Damian Hawk? You've met him, right?"

"I have. But I don't know him well."

"Where were you when you met him?"

"Umm," Wyatt tried to recall where he was when he met the famous NBA player. H was off the elevator and walking through the almost-empty offices of Dawson & Hancock. "I think I was at the opening night of this Broadway show…" He stopped. "Wait, Alexa, I think I have an idea. Let me reach out to a friend. I'll be in touch later."

Alexa squealed. "I knew you'd think of something!"

"Don't get your hopes up."

"I won't!" But her second squeal of excitement said otherwise.

Wyatt rolled his eyes; he shouldn't have told her anything until he was sure. Before he got caught up in work requests, he scrolled through the contacts on his phone and clicked on Sam Stafford's name. This was a long shot, but Wyatt realized he'd met Damian at the opening night for *LadyBird*. He was hoping Sam knew the point guard, or at least knew of a way to get in touch with him.

"Sam, it's Wyatt. How are you?"

"Wyatt! It was great seeing you last night."

"It was good to see you, too. Look, I need to ask you for a favor."

"Okay, what's up?"

"At the opening night of *LadyBird*, I met Damian Hawk. Do you know him well?"

"I'm afraid I don't know him well. The public relations firm we hired for the show took care of flooding the opening night with celebrities. You know how that is—everyone wants their photo on Page Six of the *Post*."

"Not everyone," Wyatt joked.

"Right! Not Wyatt Dawson," Sam chuckled. "What is it you need from Damian Hawk?"

Wyatt's heart sank. Looked like another dead end. "It sounds silly, but my nephew is a big fan, and the only thing he wants for Christmas is an autographed Damian Hawk basketball."

"That doesn't sound silly at all. It's Christmas! Let me think. Who reps him, do you know?"

"No idea, but I could look into it."

"I know a lot of the agents in the city. If you find out who represents him, I might be able to help you out."

Wyatt heard a woman's voice through the line. "I apologize, you're with someone. Let me stop taking up your time."

"It's fine, really," Sam laughed. "Liana and I are out for breakfast. She's giving me a hard time about being on my phone, even though she does the same thing."

"I totally understand." Wyatt leaned back and smiled, happy for his friend. "Go give Liana your full attention. I'll get back to you if I find anything out about the Hawk management team."

When they hung up, Wyatt felt good about having one more option for trying to get in touch with Hawk. He picked up his office phone. "Alice?"

"Good morning, Wyatt. You got in early today. Would you like some coffee?"

"That would be great," Wyatt said, looking at his empty cup. "And can you do me a favor and find out who represents Damian Hawk? Which agent?"

Wyatt brought his computer screen to life and when he saw the number of unopened emails, his eyes grew large. They would have to be his first task. He took a hearty sip from his fresh cup of coffee for fuel, and dove in. It was going to be a long day.

Sometime between emails, conference calls, and a client meeting in the office board room, Wyatt was able to squeeze in a quick lunch. He ate a sandwich at his desk and asked Alice to bring him another coffee. Attempting to savor his few minutes of peace, he opened the newspaper he had gotten that morning but hadn't had time to read. He chewed a bit of his sandwich as he skimmed through the pages. When his eyes caught a familiar face, he stopped mid-chew in shock. There he was, in a Page Six photo, sitting with his client Danielle Owens. The caption read:

New York City's Most Eligible Bachelor Update!

Wyatt felt sick. He put down his sandwich and read the entire blurb several times. Who was taking these photos and passing them along to the *Post*? And even more importantly, had Isabella seen this? His blood boiled with anger. If Isabella thought he was seeing other people it might have scared her away. Maybe that was why she hadn't reached out to him?

"Mr. Dawson." Alice's voice came through his intercom. "From what I understand, the ESR Agency represents Damian Hawk. I'm still trying to find out which agent exactly. I have a call into a contact there, but they haven't gotten back to me yet. I will let you know as soon as I hear back."

Wyatt slumped back in his chair. "Great."

"And also, Danielle Owens is on line two."

He took a calming breath, picked up the phone, and pressed line two. "Danielle, how are you?"

"Not great, Wyatt. Did you see today's *Post*?"

"I'm looking at it now. I apologize, Danielle, I have no idea who took this photo or how it got sent to the paper."

"This doesn't look good for my case, Wyatt, if people think we're seeing each other."

"I understand. I will call the *Post* and have them write an apology. And I'll find out who sent this to them."

"I hate to say this, but I think you may need to look at your team. Especially the few who were at lunch with us."

He paused. "I know you're upset, but let's not jump to conclusions. I can't imagine one of my team members doing something like this."

"If I were you, I wouldn't rule anyone out. People have their own ulterior motives. Even people you think you can trust." When he didn't respond, she continued. "I expect a resolution to this today. And if you discover that the source is someone who works for you, I expect them to be terminated, effective immediately."

"I will get to the bottom of it, Danielle. I can guarantee you that."

Once Danielle hung up the phone, he looked at the rest of his sandwich and his stomach turned. He pushed it away. His appetite was now gone. He paced his office, performing a mental rundown of every member of his team, with extra focus on the few who were at the lunch. It was hard to imagine any of them betraying him this way. This was the absolute worst day for something like this to happen. He didn't have time for it. He needed to find that gift for his nephew, he had a slew of afternoon meetings, and he wanted to go to The Book Nook to see Marney and find out if that was where Isabella worked.

An idea came to him and rushed to his desk in two long strides. He picked up his office phone to make a call.

"Marissa, it's Wyatt. Can you come to my office as soon as you have a minute?"

In her office, Marissa tightened her grip on the phone receiver. He either wanted to see her about finding Isabella or about the article in the newspaper, and she didn't want to talk to him about either of those topics. Unfortunately, it was time to face the music. She took a deep breath, straightened her shift dress, and confidently walked toward Wyatt's office.

"Marissa, thank you for coming immediately. I know you're busy this time of year," he said as he showed her to a seat in front of his desk.

"Of course. I see you're making progress getting into the Christmas spirit." She pointed at the little Christmas tree sitting in the corner behind his desk.

"They were selling those down the block and, you know, I felt bad for the guy standing out in the cold. I figured I would help him out. 'Tis the season, as they say."

Marissa smiled and her eyes scanned the office to see if any other holiday cheer had found its way into the room. She didn't find any other Christmas décor, but her breath caught in her throat when she saw a little framed photo sitting on his desk right next to his computer. Inside the frame was the photo from the newspaper of Wyatt and Ella Martinez. She felt sick when she saw it. He finally falls for a woman, and she's a total fraud. She was surprised he could be fooled so easily.

"What is it you wanted to talk to me about?" Marissa managed to squeak out.

Wyatt leaned back in his chair; his hands clasped together on his lap. "That's why I've always respected you, Marissa, you're direct and to the point."

She nodded and smiled weakly.

"I'll get right to it. Did you see today's *Post*?"

If Marissa said she hadn't it would make her appear incompetent, since part of her job was to stay current with New York City's happenings. However, if she said she had seen it, he would wonder why she hadn't reached out to him. In the split second she had to decide, she went with the latter of the two options.

"I did see it. I've been meaning to talk to you about it, but I've been busy all day."

"As you can imagine, I'm very upset about it. And Danielle Owens is very upset about it. It looks unprofessional and has the potential to compromise her case. You know more than anyone that perception is reality. We can't have the general public believing I'm seeing a client in that way. Do you agree?"

Marissa nodded.

"Okay, good. I want you to call your contact at the *Post*. I want you to go down to their offices and talk to him in person. Find out who's running these photos and articles and threaten legal action if there isn't a full retraction in tomorrow's paper. They at least need to give us an apology." The day's frustration had been simmering below the surface and now as he talked about the photo in the newspaper, it started to boil over.

This wasn't the first time Marissa and Wyatt had disagreed on a strategy. The difference this time was that Wyatt didn't know this *was* a strategy. He trusted her so much, he hadn't even considered that she was the one sending the photos to the *Post*. She was the one who had come up with the entire "New York City's Most Eligible Bachelor" idea. Henry, her friend at the *Post,* was not going to be happy when she made him apologize for an article she told him to run. This was quite a predicament, even for her. The wheels in her mind were spinning and she decided she would bring Henry a box of his favorite pastries from Pierre and Michelle, the famous French bakery. The decadent pastries would hopefully soften the blow.

Whenever she started to doubt her strategy, Marissa thought about who Ella Martinez *really* was, and it was all she needed to justify her actions. In the end it was all about protecting Wyatt and this firm. That was her job, and she was darn good at it.

Marissa nodded her head in agreement with everything Wyatt was ranting about. She acted angry and exasperated at the nerve of the *Post* to print such rubbish, and then left him with a promise there would be a giant apology in tomorrow's paper. Her performance had been worth of an Academy Award, but it must have done the trick. She marched out of the office with such flare, he never even had a chance to mention Isabella's name.

Now that the newspaper article was taken care of, Wyatt was ready to move on to the next item on his list: looking into Damian Hawk's agent at the ESR Agency. He had a few contacts there whom he could call and ask. He only needed to attend what felt like twenty meetings before he'd have time to call, though.

His afternoon was hectic and every time he had a spare moment he thought about Isabella. Her eyes. The smell of her perfume, which was the perfect combination of flowers and vanilla. The way she laughed shyly, covering her mouth and squinting her eyes. The Book Nook and all it represented was foremost on his mind. If he weren't as disciplined, he would have skipped work altogether and waited outside the bookstore until it opened. His anticipation grew with each passing minute. But first, work.

When it was almost 8 p.m., after most of his staff had left, he was finally able to turn off his computer and leave the office. He hoped the bookstore was still open. He got in an elevator and did his best to wait patiently as it slowly made its way down to the ground floor.

Jacob the night guard had already started his shift. As Wyatt was passing by the security desk, he bumped into Marissa who was coming toward him.

"Hi Jacob," Wyatt said, smiling and nodding at the guard, who smiled back. He turned to Marissa. "Hi, are you headed back up to the office?"

"I am. I've been at the *Post* headquarters for much too long, and still need to wrap a few things up at my desk before going home for the day."

"How did things go at the paper?"

"They went okay. I think I got my point across. They will run an apology in tomorrow's paper and there will be no more mention of 'New York City's Most Eligible Bachelor.'"

"Great, thank you. I really appreciate you going to bat for me and the firm. You look tired. You should try and get home."

Marissa nodded and took out her badge to flash to Jacob. As Wyatt was turning around to leave, he heard Jacob ask, "Ms. Mulvaney, did you ever find Ella that night you were asking about her?"

Wyatt felt the room spin. The air around him changed. He whipped around and he and Marissa stared at each other, both their faces still with shock.

"What did Jacob ask you?" Wyatt asked in a stiff and angry tone. He marched toward Marissa.

"It's not what you think, Wyatt."

"Did you discover Isabella's identity and not tell me?"

She opened her mouth to defend herself, but no words came.

"How could you do that? Withholding that information when you knew how badly I wanted to find her?" Disbelief and disappointment dripped from his every word.

"Wyatt, you don't understand."

"No, I don't." But suddenly it all became clear. "You're the one who leaked the photos to the newspaper too, aren't you?" He looked up at the ceiling, shaking his head as it all came together.

"And the New York City Most Eligible Bachelor story—that was you, too." He snorted. "How could I have been this blind? To not realize that one of my closest team members would be the one betraying me."

Marissa was shaken but she wasn't going down without a fight. "Let me explain. Please."

"I thought the bachelor story would be good for the firm. It was positive, free publicity for you and for the Christmas party. You had no date for the party. What was I supposed to do? And it worked, too! The article caused a frenzy among single women in the city. You were the talk of the town!"

"I don't want to be the talk of the town! Not for my social life, anyway. You should know that about me."

"I know, you're right. I'm sorry. And it backfired in more ways than you know."

Wyatt's head was spinning now. "What does that mean?"

"It's, well...Isabella isn't who you think she is. She..."

He held his hand up to stop Marissa from continuing. "Don't you dare. Don't say another word. I am sorry I ever got you involved in looking for Isabella. It was unprofessional, and that's my fault. But leaking photos to the press and fabricating stories about my personal life—that's unforgiveable. I'm afraid I can't trust you anymore, Marissa."

Her eyes grew wide, and her will alone kept the tears from falling. "What are you saying?"

"I'm saying that since you're on your way up to your office right now, you should clean out your desk. I don't want to see you here tomorrow."

"You're firing me?"

Wyatt nodded; his face was cold as ice.

Marissa straightened her back and stood tall. Nodding her head once, she turned to walk away. Wyatt watched her go. But after a few steps, she spun back around. "I did it for you, Wyatt. All of it. I was trying to protect you."

Out in the cold night, Wyatt inhaled deeply. The crisp air filled his lungs. How could he have been this oblivious? He had known Marissa for years, and he had seen her scheme and manipulate. She never did anything too terrible though, and it was always in favor of the firm. But he never thought she could betray him this way.

The conversation he had earlier with Danielle Owens replayed in his brain. *"People have their own ulterior motives, even people you think you can trust."* What could have been Marissa's ulterior motive? How did she benefit from the leaked photos or from hiding Isabella's identity from him?

Before he knew it, he looked up and found himself standing in front of the cutest little bookstore he'd ever seen. The Book Nook. He'd spent the entire ten-block walk in a total brain fog. He suddenly became nervous. Could Isabella Martinez really be right behind this door? There was only one way to find out. He took a deep breath and pushed the door open and a bell chimed as he entered.

The inside of the store was warm and inviting. There were twinkle lights on the ceiling, an adorable train running through a display of children's Christmas books, and soft music playing in the background. This was exactly the type of store he'd pictured Isabella working in.

"I'll be right out," an older voice yelled to him from somewhere in the back of the store.

"It's no rush, I'll look around!" he yelled back.

Marney blew in like a tornado sweeping through a field. When she saw Wyatt, her heart soared. He was browsing through books in the Sports & Entertainment section of the store.

"Mr. Dawson!" Marney practically leaped over to him. She still moved like a dancer, even at seventy-something years old.

Wyatt turned around, a smile already lighting up his face. "Marney! I thought I told you to call me Wyatt?"

The two hugged like old friends.

"I absolutely *love* your store," he told her. "I can see how you survived in this era of Amazon and big box stores. It feels like home in here."

Marney glowed with the compliment. "Thank you so much! It is a special place."

"When I saw you at the community center, you said you wanted to talk to me about something. Is everything okay?"

She nodded. She hadn't quite decided how she was going to broach the subject if Wyatt showed up. When Ella showed her the photo of him with another woman, she was afraid he wouldn't come. Each hour that went by and he still hadn't visited made her believe he wasn't interested. But here he was, and now she wasn't sure what to say.

"Everything's fine! It's nothing like that. It's a more personal matter, actually."

Wyatt looked at her, pretending to be confused by her words. But the pounding in his chest threatened to betray his faux ignorance. She had to be talking about Isabella.

"I think you met a friend of mine..." she started to say but paused.

"Are you talking about Isabella?"

"Yes, Ella. I knew it! You remember her!" Marney jumped up, clasping her hands to her heart.

"Remember her? She's all I've been able to think about since the moment I laid eyes on her."

Marney's whole body was light with love. "And she was the reason you were at the community center?"

"Yes. I was hoping she would be there. Unfortunately, I never got the chance to see her. To be clear, we're both talking about Ella Martinez, right?

She nodded, smiling.

And she works here?"

"She does!"

"But she's not here now?"

Marney sighed. "No, she's not. She was here all day, but she left a few minutes ago. You just missed her."

Disappointment appeared on his face. She desperately wanted to tell him more. She wanted to tell him all about Ella, and

Kate Kasch

how amazing she was. Most importantly, she wanted to tell him where he could find her now. But she didn't want to betray Ella.

Wyatt looked expectantly at Marney, silently willing her to divulge more information. When she looked into his sincere, beautiful, light-hazel eyes, she caved.

"I do know where Ella is now, if you'd like to go see her?"

"Yes, please, Marney!" His whole face lit up like twinkle lights.

"She's at 430 Fifth Avenue. The 22nd floor."

Wyatt was utterly confused now. "But that's my office. Why would she be there?"

"I think you need to go see for yourself."

Chapter Twenty-Six

Ella left The Book Nook and shoved her hands in her pockets to keep warm while she walked. In her rush out the door this morning she had forgotten to bring her mittens. She felt something smooth and round in her pocket. She pulled the object out and in her palm was the rose quartz stone—the stone of unconditional love. Marney must have slipped it in her pocket before she left.

Unconditional love. Ella had experienced it before. She had felt it in her father's embrace and when her mother stroked her hair. She had been blessed to be surrounded by it at home and had never thought she needed it from anyone else. But then she met Wyatt, and everything she had once believed about love changed forever. The love of a partner, someone who would look at you longingly and want to know your deepest thoughts…that was missing in her life. That tiny hole of emptiness was blown wide open the moment she met Wyatt, and there was no way to close it now. It was a giant hole now, and it was threatening to swallow her up. And it was all her fault. She hadn't been willing to let him in. She didn't give him the chance to get to know her.

Ella was filled with mixed emotions as she arrived at 430 Fifth Avenue. Part of her felt deep sadness, and part of her felt at peace. She had learned something about herself. The flawed bits of insecurity were exposed. The lack of balance had toppled her over, but now that she knew the problem, she could fix it.

Up on the 22nd floor, she started her routine. She changed into her cleaning uniform and got her earbuds and phone ready to play some Christmas music. On her way to the storage closet to get her cleaning supplies, she wasn't paying attention and bumped right into someone coming the other way.

Marissa Mulvaney stood in front of her, looking as surprised as she was. She had a brown box resting on her hip, which was filled with folders, papers, pens, pencils, and what looked like a framed photo of herself.

Marissa laughed at the irony of the situation, but there was no joy in it. "Of course! Of course, I would run into you in here. You're here on the night shift—you're here to clean the office."

Ella stood still, unable to find any words as Marissa's apparent anger caught her off guard.

"Where's that charm and confidence that oozed out of your every pore the night of the Christmas party, huh? That was all part of your act, too?"

"What? I'm not sure what you mean," Ella somehow managed to mumble.

"Oh, now you're playing the sweet innocent cleaning lady, is that it?"

Ella was shocked. She had no response. But Marissa wasn't finished yet. She continued, each word cutting into Ella like a knife. "Once I found out who you were, I vowed to protect Wyatt from you. Despite being a sharp attorney, he can be unbelievably naïve. Your designer dress, Hollywood hair and dazzling smile may have tricked him, but not me. Let me guess, you saw the article in the paper. You saw that he was wealthy and single and decided to come after him. How did you even get into the party?"

"I found an invitation, and—" Ella started, but Marissa jumped in before she could finish.

"You found one? What, here? While you were cleaning? Ha!" Another bitter laugh. "You must have thought it was your lucky day. Cinderella getting to go to the ball and steal away the prince."

"What? No," Ella was shaking her head. "I thought…"

187

"Oh, well. It doesn't matter anymore. I'm done trying to protect Wyatt. I didn't tell him about you, but he found out your name somehow anyway. And you know what? Good luck. Let him find out for himself who you really are. Then he'll know why I did what I did."

"Marissa, that's enough!" A deep voice cut through the air.

Marissa and Ella both turned toward the voice, and there stood Wyatt. Ella felt like she had had the air knocked out of her. She couldn't breathe.

Wyatt walked closer, anger seething out of every pore. "Marissa, I was feeling bad for having fired you earlier, but now I am one hundred percent certain I made the right decision. It's time for you to leave. Now."

"Wyatt, do you see who this woman is? She cleans offices for a living! Can you imagine if the public knew you were dating the firm's maid?" Marissa asked in an exasperated tone.

"I said you could leave, Marissa. You no longer work here."

She stormed off in a huff. The box of her desk belongings bounced on her hip as she walked. Halfway down the hall, she turned back around. Her stare was as cold as the North Pole. "Don't be surprised if there is another little update on New York City's Most Eligible Bachelor in tomorrow's paper, and it won't be a flattering article for either of you!"

As Ella watched Marissa turn and go, her brain tried to keep up with everything that was happening. She turned to face Wyatt.

"Isabella," he whispered.

She tried to find her voice. "It's Ella, actually," she said, looking him in the eyes.

"Ella, I'm sorry."

"For what?"

"For everything." He moved closer to her, reaching his hand out to touch her arm. "For everything I heard Marissa say, which was awful. And for not knowing..." He looked around the office, embarrassed.

"For not knowing I clean your office?" She glanced down at her uniform and black sneakers.

He nodded, looking in her eyes so deeply that she swore he could read her thoughts.

"I'm sorry, too," she said softly. "I shouldn't have misled you the night of the Christmas party."

"Misled me? Are you telling me that the woman I spent the entire night talking to…Were those thoughts and ideas and stories you shared not really yours?"

"Well, no, I'm not saying that. I meant everything I said that night. Everything I told you was true. I guess I mean, I left a few things out."

"You didn't leave anything important out." He placed his hands on her shoulders and her skin tingled at his touch. "I know you're studying to be a teacher and are almost finished with your degree. I know you work at The Book Nook with an eccentric, sweet woman named Marney, and I know you volunteer at the Manhattan Community Center where you helped organize the most adorable Christmas play I've ever seen." He smiled down at her, and she laughed shyly.

"I know you lost your dad a few years ago and you still miss him. I know you're a good listener and have a huge heart."

Ella's eyes were wet with tears. No one had ever talked about her this way before. She didn't want to ruin the moment, but she had to ask him a question. Otherwise she would always wonder. "During your speech at the Christmas party, you said…" she made air quotes, "you said 'from the partners to the cleaning crew and everyone in between.' From where I stood, that meant the partners were at the top and the cleaning people were at the bottom. Is that how you really feel?

He was shocked that she remembered that line from his speech. "I'm sorry for saying that. I certainly didn't mean it in a derogatory way. I meant that every member of this office is an integral part of our success."

Ella looked down at her hands. "Then shouldn't the cleaning crew have been invited to the Christmas party?"

Wyatt's face flushed with embarrassment. "You're absolutely right. I'm ashamed for not including *everyone* who helps our office run. Next year, it will be different. That's a promise."

And just like that, the fact that she was a cleaning lady in Wyatt's building no longer mattered.

"And there's one more thing I know," Wyatt said softly, lifting her chin and bringing her eyes up to meet his once again. "I know that I'm in love with you." He leaned down and his lips touched hers gently. Goose bumps formed on her arms and her heart beat wildly in her chest.

As he pulled away, she needed a few seconds to collect herself before speaking again. "I'm in love with you, too," she finally whispered. "And I have one more apology. I'm sorry I hid from you at the community center." She shrugged, smiling.

Wyatt laughed. "I think it all worked out the way it was meant to. I met Marney!"

"Isn't she the greatest?"

Wyatt nodded. His face was fixed in a permanent smile. "Oh! I almost forgot!" She watched him fumble around in his coat pocket. "Is this yours?"

He held out a gold pendant. When she saw it, she gasped and brought her hand to her mouth. "My pendant! You found it?"

"I found it on the sidewalk when you rushed out of the party. It must have slipped off your neck as you were getting into the cab." He draped the necklace around her neck and secured it.

"You have no idea what this means to me. My father gave this to me, and I thought it was gone forever…" Tears once again filled Ella's eyes.

"It helped me find you. Your initials are on it."

Ella looked into his light eyes and her heart and soul were happier than she could ever remember them being. She whispered, "*Nunca dejes de sonar.*"

Chapter Twenty-Seven

Rosie seemed to appear out of nowhere and offered to handle Ella's workload for the night. When she tried to decline the offer, Rosie all but pushed her out the door with Wyatt.

She dashed back into the ladies' room and changed back into her jeans and red cashmere sweater. She let her hair down and hastily ran a brush through the thick waves. Her stomach was aflutter with joyous nerves as she dug into her handbag looking for some of the blush and lip gloss Mac had given her the night of the Christmas party.

They found a cozy Italian restaurant with a fire burning in the hearth and peaceful Christmas music playing quietly in the background. They talked like old friends who hadn't seen each other in ages as they ate plates of fresh pasta and drank glasses of red wine. At some point during their conversation, Ella asked him why his office had no personal items in it. He laughed when she told him that she and Rosie called it Scrooge's office.

"I guess I've always wanted to be sure I was focused on work. I didn't want any distractions. If my office were decorated like a home, I thought I would get too comfortable, too complacent. I wanted my office to be a reminder that I was there to work and that was it."

Ella nodded. "I can understand that. I am also guilty of being too fixated on school and work."

"Until you met me." Wyatt's eyes sparkled with delight.

"I think you put a framed photo of us in your office after you met me," Ella teased.

Wyatt shook his head. "Although I'd love to take credit, I wasn't the one who put the framed photo of us in my office."

"If not you, then who?"

Wyatt shrugged.

"I guess that'll be a Christmas mystery. But you did put up the Christmas tree, right?"

"I sure did. You turned me from Scrooge to Santa Claus. Speaking of Santa Claus, tomorrow is Christmas Eve and I haven't gotten my nephew his gift yet."

"Want me to help you? Now that school is over, I'm free until after the New Year!"

"Thank you," Wyatt said, reaching over and placing his hand gently on hers. "But I don't think you can help with this gift."

Ella looked at him curiously.

"My nephew, Michael," he began.

"That's your older sister Alexa's son?" Ella confirmed.

"Yes! Good memory. I can't even keep all my nieces and nephews straight." He smiled at her. "Michael loves basketball. All he wants for Christmas is a Damian Hawk autographed basketball. Alexa asked me to get it for him."

"Damian Hawk? The point guard for the Knicks?" Ella's eyes widened.

"That's the one. Now you see my problem."

"That is a problem. He lives in the city, and he's quite the partier from what I understand."

"He is. How do *you* know that?" he asked. Ella never ceased to surprise him.

"These girls I know from NYU, they would go to this club called Ice all the time. I never really went with them, but they would always talk about how Damian Hawk liked to hang out there. Of course, everyone was always vying for his attention. Word spread and the club became impossible to get into."

"He hangs out at Ice?" Wyatt perked up. "I know the owner of Ice. His name's Ryker Rensselaer. He's a big real estate magnate. I represented him in a lawsuit once. Great guy."

"You know the owner of Ice?" Ella tried to hide that she was impressed. "You would have been very popular at NYU," she laughed.

"I hate to do this to you, but would you mind if I made a phone call?"

"Of course not! Call him!"

Wyatt stepped away from the table to call Ryker. She sipped her wine and watched the flames dance in the fireplace. A relaxed smile was etched permanently on her face. She couldn't believe how comfortable she and Wyatt already were around each other. How silly that she hid from him this week, missing all those opportunities to be with him. At that very moment she vowed to say "yes" to any invitation to any event, despite how nervous it might make her feel or how far out of her comfort zone it took her. She didn't want to miss one more minute with him.

As he sat back down next to her, Ella looked over at him to gauge his mood. The nervous look on his face worried her.

"How did it go? Did that Ryker guy know anything about Damian Hawk?"

Wyatt leaned over and put his elbows on his knees, his hands clasped together in front of him. "Here's the thing. Ryker is not at Ice right now. He's out to dinner with his girlfriend, but he texted the manager over there and Damian is there. Right now."

Although there was no question in that statement, Ella knew what he was asking. She stood up, never taking her eyes off him. "Well, let's go."

A huge smile lit up Wyatt's face, and he stood up and wrapped her in a warm hug. "Where have you been all my life?" He whispered into her ear.

"I've been cleaning your office," she deadpanned. They both burst into laughter.

The slow, relaxed night suddenly turned into a rushed, adrenaline-filled adventure. Wyatt paid the bill while Ella retrieved their coats. After bundling up, they stepped outside into the crisp December air. Ella shivered and Wyatt put his arm around her.

"We need a cab." He walked over to the curb and held his arm out to signal to the passing taxis to stop. When one finally did, the two hopped in and the heat inside the car warmed their skin.

"To the nearest sporting goods store, please," he told the driver. He turned to Ella. "We need a basketball!"

"That would be…" the driver had to think for a minute. "Dawson's Sporting Goods. Will that work?"

Ella whipped her head around to look at him, her eyes wide. "Don't even tell me that's your family's company."

"Let's save that conversation for another day," Wyatt said, looking rather sheepish. She nodded her head slowly, not quite sure she was ready to know all about the Dawson family business, anyway.

The cab pulled up in front of the sporting goods store, and Wyatt looked at the dark windows and then at his watch. "I don't think it's open. It's pretty late."

Ella looked around at the stores around them, trying to think of another option. When she couldn't think of anything she asked, "You don't have some kind of master key to all the Dawson Sporting Goods stores?"

Wyatt shook his head. "My siblings might, but I definitely don't. No way my dad would give me that kind of access."

"Could you call one of your siblings? See if they could help?"

Wyatt stared at the store. His mind was running through all his options. He could try calling Alexa, although it was late on a Friday night and she would most likely be asleep.

"Wait! There's someone in there!" Ella yelled. "Over there!" She pointed at one of the front doors, and they could see someone vacuuming inside. They hopped out of the cab, ran up to the doors and started banging on them. Ella felt bad; she didn't want to startle the man who was vacuuming. Rosie had certainly startled her enough times that way, but she also realized that this was their best chance at finding a basketball at this time of night.

They kept banging on the door and waving their hands in the air until the man finally saw them. He looked at them skeptically, unsure what these two crazy people who were jumping up and down in the street could want from a sporting goods store. He cautiously walked toward the door and yelled through the glass in broken English. "What you want?"

"Show him your license!" Ella told Wyatt "Let him see your last name."

Wyatt held his license up to the door, pointing at it and repeatedly saying "Dawson," but the man didn't seem to make the connection. Wyatt yelled through the glass again. "Can we come in? My family owns the store!" But the man looked at them like they had escaped from the funny farm.

Right when Ella was about to give up, she thought of something else, and tried one more time. *"Hola! Mi nombre es Ella y este es Wyatt Dawson. La familia de Wyatt es dueña de la tienda. Necesitamos comprar una pelota de baloncesto como regalo para su sobrino—para Navidad. Muy importante. ¿Podemos entrar? Muy importante."*

The city blurred around him as Wyatt stared at Ella. His jaw dropped open in awe as he listened to her communicate with the man in the store. After a little more discussion, she and the man were laughing through the glass like old friends. The man held up a finger to signal he would be right back. He left, and in less than a minute he was back at the front door, unlocking it for them. He had a big smile on his face.

"Gracias," Wyatt said to the man awkwardly, holding out his hand for a handshake.

"His name is Jose," Ella whispered to Wyatt.

He tried again. "Gracias, Jose." He turned to Ella. "Can you tell him how grateful I am and how much this means to me? And tell him I will let the store manager know that he helped us out."

"I told him," Ella smiled and walked into the store. "I also told him we would get him a Damian Hawk autographed basketball."

Wyatt shook his head in disbelief, chuckling as he followed her in.

"Where are the basketballs?" Ella asked.

Less than five minutes later, with two basketballs in their hands and after many thanks to Jose, Ella and Wyatt were ready for part two of their Christmas gift adventure. They hailed a second cab, giggling as they got in at how silly they looked holding basketballs. It was a quick ride down to Ice and they stepped out of the cab still laughing at themselves.

"Uh oh." Ella's face fell as she looked at the scene in front of them.

"What?" Wyatt followed her gaze. "Wow, that's a lot of people."

The club's sign was a backlit steel rectangle with the letters *I* -*C* -*E* etched into it. It was modern and sleek, which most likely mirrored the interior decor. That was not the problem, though. The problem was that outside the two hulking steel doors of the club was a line of people, all wearing Santa hats, snaking down the street. The line itself had become a scene right there on the sidewalk. While they waited to get in, everyone was talking and laughing, and a few people were even dancing. Ella turned to Wyatt with a confused look on her face as if to ask, "What is going on?"

When they made eye contact, they burst out laughing once again.

"Did your friend, the owner of the club, mention anything to you about a Santa theme at the club tonight?"

Wyatt shook his head. "He didn't. He also didn't mention a line down the block."

"Should we try and wait in line?"

"No way. It'll take all night!" Wyatt's eyes scanned the line. "Let me see what I can do."

He handed Ella the basketball he was holding, and she giggled as she tried to hold both. He laughed too. "You got it?"

She nodded.

Full of confidence and swagger, Wyatt strode over to the two bulky guys working the front door. The two men were as big as boulders with muscles bulging under their black t-shirts. They didn't wear jackets, despite the frigid temperature. The words, *cold as ICE* were spelled out across the shirts, the letters stretching across their rippling chests.

Ella watched Wyatt have a conversation with the men. After a minute, he waved to her. Holding a basketball on each hip, she scurried over to them.

"Here, put these on," one of the bouncers said, handing Wyatt and Ella each a Santa hat. "And be cool when you go in. I don't want a riot out here. Some of these people have already been in line for hours."

Wyatt and Ella nodded as they put on their Santa hats, which wasn't an easy thing to do while holding basketballs.

"And you can't bring those in." The bouncer pointed at the balls.

"We have to bring them in. It's the reason we're here." Ella's voice stayed firm, despite her anxiety.

"Please man, this is for my nephew's Christmas present," Wyatt pleaded. "You don't want to ruin a kid's Christmas, do you?"

The man stared straight ahead, keeping his eyes on the line. He slowly slid his gaze to the other bouncer and the two seemed to have a silent conversation. After what seemed like an unusually long time, he glanced sideways at Wyatt. "Okay, go ahead. But if anyone asks, I didn't allow it."

"Thank you! You have no idea what this means to us!" Ella gushed.

If the bouncer heard her, he didn't let on. His expression stayed cold as ice, as he continued to stare straight ahead. Wyatt and Ella took that as their cue and slipped through the heavy front doors.

Inside the club, Ella could feel the loud, pulsing music pounding in her chest. "Is that techno Christmas music?" she yelled to Wyatt. Even though he was right in front of her, he still couldn't hear a word she was saying. He grabbed her free hand, the other one still holding a basketball, and led her through the crushing mass of dancing club-goers. Bodies were crammed onto the dance floor, as lights flashed to the beat of the music. The whole scene was a reminder to Ella why she didn't like clubs like this. She could feel a headache coming on.

Once across the dance floor they stepped up into a clearing and Ella felt like she could breathe again. There were platforms containing roped-off tables and each area appeared to have its own server. It was the VIP area. Ella followed Wyatt's gaze as he searched each of the tables, looking for Damian Hawk. He was all the way up the stairs and to the right, in the largest private seating area. It had an L-shaped couch and three small tables full of candles and buckets of champagne. He sat there like a King on his throne, surrounded by admirers.

It was still too loud to talk to each other. Wyatt pointed up at the area to show Ella where they were headed. She nodded in response. Much to her relief, the noise dissipated the further up they went. When they reached the top of the stairs, another hulking man in a black *cold as ICE* t-shirt was standing guard.

Wyatt leaned in toward the security guard and tried to explain why he and Ella were there. Ella didn't know what he said or how the security guard responded, but she saw the man shake his head as if saying no. It wasn't a good sign. He tried again, leaning closer and gesturing with his free hand. The security guard once more shook his head no.

Wyatt looked back at Ella with a worried expression. She looked past the guard at the couch full of people. Damian Hawk was all the way at the back, making it hard for her to even see him. To get here, they'd sweet talked a nice man to let them into a closed store, carried basketballs all over the city, and wore Santa hats to get inside this insane club. They'd come too far to leave empty-handed now. Determined, she did the only thing she could think of.

"Damian! Damian Hawk!" she yelled, waving her free arm at him.

At that point the security guard tried to usher Wyatt and Ella back down the stairs. But suddenly they heard someone yell back, "Wyatt! Wyatt Dawson!"

Damian Hawk stood up and like the Red Sea parting, everyone in his vicinity moved aside so he could walk over to where Ella, Wyatt and the scowling security guard stood.

Standing at about 6'8", Damian was a giant. His smile was wide and friendly, and he tapped the guard on the shoulder. "Pauly, they cool. They with me."

Pauly stepped aside and let Wyatt and Ella into the VIP area. Damian fist-bumped Wyatt, and then did that half hug, half back-slap thing that guys do. Laughing, he greeted his friend. "Wyatt Dawson at ICE? I must have had too much champagne!"

"It's a Christmas miracle!" Wyatt laughed too. "This is Ella Martinez. Ella this is Damian Hawk."

Damian practically had to bend in half to do it, but he wrapped Ella in a giant hug. "You know you're with a legend, right?" Assuming that the basketball star was referring to himself, Ella nodded her head enthusiastically.

"Wyatt Dawson, man. He is a legend," Damian continued. She looked back and forth from Wyatt to Damian, confused. "That's right. Some shady guy tried to sue the Knicks for something bogus, and my man Wyatt swooped in and saved the day! Saved our whole season!"

"I had no idea!" Ella said, turning to Wyatt with a smile on her face. Her eyes sparkled with pride. "He is quite a surprise."

"That he is!" Damian agreed. "Come, sit down! Have a glass of champagne!"

Ella and Wyatt both shook their heads. "Thank you, but we really can't stay," Wyatt told him. "We actually need a favor."

Wyatt explained that his nephew's Christmas wish was for an autographed ball. He then went on to tell the story of how they ended up in the club, and why they needed a second autograph for the kind man who had helped them with their project.

"Of course, man. For you?" Damian said. "I'll give you as many autographed balls as you need." He turned to someone at the table behind them. "Cory! You got a Sharpie?"

Apparently, Damian getting asked for his autograph was a regular thing. So much so, that he had a friend who always brought extra pens. He signed the basketballs with a flourish, and then held them both in his giant hands. With a mischievous smile, he looked back and forth between Wyatt and Ella. "Before I give you these, you have to do one thing for me."

The look on Damian's face made Wyatt hesitate to answer.

"You have to come dance." Damian smiled wide.

Wyatt and Ella tried to decline again. They looked down at the daunting dance floor, which from their vantage point looked like nothing more than a sea of red hats bouncing to the beat.

"I insist! One dance. Come on. It's Christmas!"

It was clear Damian wasn't going to take no for an answer. He handed the basketballs to Pauly, and led the way to the stairs, already starting to dance on his way down. Ella and Wyatt looked at each other and shrugged. They took off their coats and followed him down. The DJ was playing some sort of Christmas song remix that had barely recognizable versions of "Rockin' Around the Christmas Tree" and "Jingle Bell Rock" mashed together.

When they had made their way down to the dance floor, Ella and Wyatt looked at each other and burst into laughter. Ella shrugged again, since the noise level made talking out of the question. She started to dance. Wyatt paused for a moment to watch her before joining in. Damian Hawk, was nearby, towering over everyone. He saw them and flashed them a thumbs-up. Ella got caught up in the energy of the crowd and was surprised at how much she was enjoying herself. For the first time in maybe forever, she felt truly carefree. Wyatt looked happier than she had ever seen him before. Despite the crowded dance floor, she felt like she and Wyatt were alone. They didn't take their eyes off each other as their bodies moved to the pulsing music.

When the song ended and a new one began, Ella looked up and saw Damian pointing up the stairs. He started to climb them, and Ella and Wyatt followed. Their cheeks were flushed, and they were slightly out of breath. At the top, he handed them the two basketballs. "Merry Christmas, man. And you call me anytime you need something, okay?"

They thanked Damian and wished him a Merry Christmas. Ella gave him another hug. Wyatt led them back through the sea of people and somehow, they found their way to the front doors. Never had Ella thought the streets of New York City could be described as calm, but as she burst through that door, she was thankful for fresh air and quiet. Her cheeks were still flushed from the dancing, and her ears were ringing. She looked at Wyatt and she smiled so hard her cheeks hurt.

"That was the most amazing experience I've ever had," she confessed.

"Definitely not my typical Friday night," Wyatt said, laughing.

They started walking down the sidewalk in a comfortable silence, unsure of what to do next.

"It's pretty late. I should probably head home," Ella told him. They stopped and looked at each other and Wyatt reached for her hand.

"I guess you're right, but I don't want this night to end."

"Me neither." Ella smiled. "But tomorrow is Christmas Eve!"

"That's right, it is. Do you have big plans?"

Ella chuckled. "No. My mom and I make pastelillos and sazon and we sip coquitos while watching Christmas movies, of course . . ."

Wyatt held up his hand, signaling Ella to pause, "I'm dying to know -- what are pastelillos and coquitos?"

"It's traditional Puerto Rican food, we do it to honor my dad. Pastelillos are kind of like empanadas stuffed with meat, and sazon is yellow rice and beans. But my absolute favorite is the coquitos." Ella got excited as she thought about the tasty treats. "A coquito is almost like a coconut eggnog – it's amazing."

"Wow, I've never heard of any of those foods! Would you make them for me some time?"

"I would love too." Ella blushed with delight. "How about you? You said you don't usually go home to Connecticut, right?"

His face lit up. "I just had the best idea!"

Chapter Twenty-Eight

"How's this dress?" Ella asked her mom as she stepped out of the changing room wearing a long silver gown.

"Oh, my goodness! That's the most beautiful dress I've ever seen. That's the one, absolutely!"

Whether her mom was being honest or was tired of watching her daughter try on what seemed like thousands of dresses, Ella wasn't sure. But either way the silver dress was her favorite, too.

"I'm lucky my mom works at Leighton's," Ella said, smiling at her mom. Regina had asked permission from her boss to shop in the store before it opened on that Saturday morning, which also happened to be Christmas Eve. With mocha lattes in hand, the two women walked into the store giggling like teenagers on their first shopping spree. Ella had decided that since she was no longer a student and was about to be a teacher, it was time to update her wardrobe. And besides, she needed a dress for the impromptu Christmas Eve party she and Wyatt had decided to throw that evening.

Ella was functioning on only a few hours of sleep and was fueled solely by excitement and coffee. She felt like her entire life had changed in the last twenty-four hours. The thought that last night was only the second time she and Wyatt had been together blew her mind. It was as if every event in her life up until this week had led her to him. All the good things, and even all the not-so-good things, had prepared her to be with him. And tonight, they were already throwing their first holiday party together.

After shopping until she dropped, Ella rushed home to prepare for the party. Regina stayed on at Leighton's since she still had to work half a day. After a quick shower, Ella dressed in jeans and a sweater, and gathered up her new dress and shoes. Once outside, her apartment, she struggled to figure out how she was going to carry everything on the train. At that moment a black sedan pulled up in front of her and man with a full head of gray hair stepped out from the driver's side. "Isabella Martinez?" he asked calmly.

She nodded slowly.

"Wyatt Dawson sent me to pick you up. He said you might need a lift to his apartment?"

Ella gasped. How on earth was she this lucky?

It was a smooth ride into Manhattan and up Fifth Avenue to Wyatt's apartment overlooking Central Park. She spent most of the ride on her phone, calling her friends to invite them to the party. She also called in a favor to Rosie's husband, Ernesto. He was a caterer, and Ella begged him to provide the food. He was sweet and soft-spoken—Rosie's polar opposite, but perhaps that's why they say opposites attract. Ernesto didn't stand a chance when it came to Ella begging him to serve some traditional Puerto Rican dishes. He agreed, and even offered to make a large punch bowl of coquito. For Ella, it wasn't Christmas Eve without that sweet drink.

The driver, Jeffrey, pulled the sedan up in front of the front door to Wyatt's building and a doorman in a sharp gray uniform immediately walked up to open the door for her.

"Ms. Martinez? Let me help you with your bags."

She followed the doorman into the grand limestone building. "Mr. Dawson is in Penthouse Four, you can go on up. He's expecting you."

Ella smiled and thanked him. As the elevator ascended smoothly up toward the penthouse, Ella tried to relax and appear unimpressed by the level of luxury with which Wyatt appeared to live. Suddenly, the elevator stopped, and the doors opened to reveal the foyer in Wyatt's apartment.

He walked up to meet her, dressed casually in crisp denim and a striped button-down shirt with the sleeves rolled up. Their eyes met and they smiled shyly at each other. Throwing caution to the wind, he grabbed her in a bear hug, lifting her off the ground. She closed her eyes, taking in his scent and savoring the feeling of his body close to hers. When she opened her eyes, she froze. "Uh oh."

Gently placing her back on the ground, Wyatt looked at her questioningly. "What? What's wrong?"

"Your apartment."

"You don't like my apartment?" Wyatt chuckled a little.

"No, it's not that. Your apartment is gorgeous." She looked around at the vast living area. The whole back wall was floor-to-ceiling windows which overlooked Central Park. "We're having a Christmas Eve party here in a few hours and you don't even have a Christmas tree!"

"Hmmm, I see what you mean. But I don't really do the whole Christmas tree thing."

Ella dropped her bags on a chair. "Get your coat on. We're going Christmas shopping."

After a few hours of shopping, they had bought a Christmas tree which was being delivered that afternoon, tree ornaments, a wreath for the front door, about a million twinkle lights, and yards and yards of garland. Jeffrey drove them around from store to store, blasting Christmas music in the car at Ella's request. At first Ella had been concerned that Wyatt's apartment was completely devoid of Christmas décor, but she was having so much fun shopping she was happy it had worked out that way.

Every available space in the car was packed with shopping bags. Ella and Wyatt laughed when they looked at each other; they were both up to their necks in garland in the back seat.

"Do you think we have enough?" Wyatt chuckled.

"We just did years of Christmas decoration shopping in one afternoon. But I think we were very successful!"

Back at the apartment, they looked around at the sea of shopping bags and were overwhelmed by the sheer volume. "Where do we even start?" Wyatt asked.

The intercom buzzed. "Mr. Dawson, you have a Christmas tree delivery. Can I let them up?"

"Yes, please," Wyatt confirmed. And then to Ella, "We need to make room for the tree!"

"The tree should go there," Ella pointed to the center of the room where a chair sat. "It should be center stage – the star of the show. Could you move that chair out of the way?"

Wyatt did as he was asked. Two men brought the Christmas tree into the apartment and put it where Ella showed them. Once the tree was in place, she looked to Wyatt to see what he thought.

"It's perfect," he said, smiling at her.

Ella looked at her phone. "We don't have much time; we need to get moving. I'll go hang the wreath; you start unraveling the garland."

They listened to more Christmas music as they decorated. Ella and Wyatt moved through the apartment, draping garland and hanging twinkle lights. The sun faded into dusk and the apartment was glowing. When the shopping bags were empty and all the decorations were out, they plopped down on the sofa, exhausted.

"It's magical," Ella said as she looked around at what they'd done.

Wyatt nodded in agreement. "I had no idea my apartment could look like this."

"Wait!" She jumped up. "We need to turn on the Christmas tree."

"I didn't hang lights on the tree, did you?" Wyatt asked her.

Ella's eyes grew wide in panic, "No. Oh no, how did we forget about the tree?"

They stared at the beautiful, albeit bare, tree in the center of the room.

She looked at her phone again. "There's no time now, the guests will be arriving soon, and we need to get changed."

"Maybe no one will notice?" Wyatt said. He and Ella looked at each other, then looked at the looming pine tree in the living room and burst into laughter.

"Oh well, we tried," Ella shrugged.

The intercom buzzed again. This time it was the caterer. Wyatt let them up and a four people from Ernesto's crew started to set up the food and beverages in the kitchen, which opened to the living room.

In the guest room, Ella changed into her long silver gown. She let her hair down from the bun that had been in all day and used the curling iron the way Jackie taught her to curl the ends of her hair. She took her time to swipe on blush and mascara and added a shimmery shadow on her eyelids. Lastly, she applied a red lipstick and put on dangling sparkly earrings. She slipped on the glittery shoes she had bought that morning at Leighton's and stared at her reflection in the mirror. She had come a long way in the last week.

Wyatt sat at the kitchen island overlooking the living room. He wore a navy suit, tailored perfectly to his long, lean body, with a crisp white shirt that was open at the collar. When Ella emerged from the guest room, he stood up. His eyes were smoldering at the sight of her. "You look amazing," he whispered hoarsely.

Ella walked toward him, smiling. "Thank you. You clean up nicely, as well."

"I don't think anyone will notice the Christmas tree. You will be the glowing star tonight." Ella blushed at his compliment.

"Here, I poured us a glass of champagne." Wyatt handed Ella a crystal flute of the bubbly beverage and took one for himself. "A toast," he said as they clinked glasses. "To you, Isabella Martinez, and to the best Christmas I've ever had."

Ella sipped her champagne. "And it's only Christmas Eve!"

As if on cue, the buzzer rang, and the elevator door dinged. The doors opened, and a large group of people filled the living room. There was already chatter and laughter as Marney, Rosie, Liana and Sam entered the room. Once they saw the beautiful apartment and Wyatt and Ella standing together looking fabulous, all the noise stopped as they took in the scene.

Marney was the first to come back to life. "Ella! My goodness, this is beautiful." She looked around the room. "*You* are beautiful!"

Marney's exclamation broke the ice, and everyone quickly followed suit. There was chatter and laughter as the guests all greeted the hosts and each other. Servers started passing around flutes filled with the creamy coquito. Regina, Bonnie, Jackie, Mac and the rest of the glam squad were the next group of guests to arrive, as well as some of Wyatt's friends and co-workers. The atmosphere was festive and fun.

Ella grabbed a few strings of lights and handed them to Sam and Marney. They started wrapping the tree with them. Liana and Bonnie opened boxes of ornaments. Soon the whole party was decorating the tree together as they sang along to Christmas songs. Marney even convinced Wyatt to dance with her.

"I have danced twice in two days," Wyatt said to Ella after he somehow escaped Marney's clutches, "and my apartment looks like a Christmas movie. I think this is the year of firsts for me."

Ella laughed.

"Not to mention I have the most amazing woman to spend this Christmas with." He wrapped his arms around her waist. "Did you see what I bought at the store while you weren't looking?" He pointed up toward the ceiling where a sprig of mistletoe dangled above them. He leaned down and kissed Ella's lips gently. Her whole body felt like it was melting to his touch.

"Okay you two lovebirds, break it up," Marney teased them. She and Bonnie were standing there rolling their eyes at them. "I need to steal Ella for a minute."

Reluctantly, Ella followed Marney and Bonnie into the kitchen.

"Is everything okay?" Ella asked.

The two women smiled and nodded at her, bursting with anticipation. "We had the best idea!" Marney said.

"Great! What?"

"I know who can replace you at The Book Nook when you start your teaching job," Bonnie said, lighting up with excitement.

"Really? Who?"

"Joana!" the two women said in unison.

"Joana?" Ella asked. "Is she old enough?"

"She recently turned fourteen, which is the legal working age in New York," Bonnie explained.

"Joana will be the perfect fit!" Ella exclaimed. "Marney, you are going to absolutely love her. She's a hard worker, and just the sweetest!"

"Didn't I tell you that everything always works out the way it's supposed to?"

Chapter Twenty-Nine

"Come on, Mom!" Ella yelled to Regina from the kitchen. "He's here!"

Regina rushed in from her bedroom pulling a suitcase behind her.

"I think you're worse than me with the packing," Ella teased her mom.

"I do work at a department store, you know. And of course, I had to buy gifts for all of Wyatt's nieces and nephews."

"I told you I was buying them all gifts," Ella looked at her mother, bewildered. "Then I guess they'll have lots of gifts, won't they?" Regina shrugged as Ella rolled her eyes. "When was the last time we had young girls and boys to spoil at Christmastime? Don't be such a scrooge!"

"Very funny, Mom. Ready to go?" Ella asked, putting on her long, white cashmere coat. Ella had worn this coat more in the past two weeks than it had been worn in the past twenty years combined. It was part of the life balance that she had been working on ever since she met Wyatt.

They locked up their apartment and met Wyatt, who was standing by the car, waiting for them.

"Merry Christmas, Martinez ladies," Wyatt said, smiling. He was wearing dark jeans, a grayish-blue sweater, and a long navy overcoat. Ella looked at him leaning against his sleek, dark sedan and her heart danced.

"Merry Christmas." She gave him a warm hug and a peck on the cheek.

The luggage was stored in the trunk, and all three settled in the car. They were off!

"Everyone ready for a chaotic Christmas in Connecticut?" Wyatt asked.

"Nothing could be better than a loud and crazy Christmas filled with children and family. It reminds me of when I was growing up." Regina smiled.

"I agree. I think my mom and I have had enough quiet Christmases. We're ready for some fun!" Ella looked over at Wyatt. "Did you remember the basketball?"

"Of course, I did!" He may have sounded carefree, but she knew better. This was a big deal for him, and he was nervous. The last time he had been home for the holidays, years ago, he and his father had fought, and Wyatt's father had told him to leave. And Ella was pretty sure he had never brought a girlfriend home with him. Her stomach flipped with nerves.

They needed a distraction, so she picked up the newspaper that was folded on the car console and started to read.

"Ha!" Ella laughed as she read.

"What is it?" Wyatt asked.

"Listen to this." Ella read aloud from the paper:

Liana Lapierre and Sam Stafford Team Up to Save Manhattan Community Center

Famed fashion designer, Liana Lapierre, together with Broadway director Sam Stafford, have not only been hot and heavy in New York's social scene this holiday season, they have also made large donations to save a community center in Harlem that was scheduled to close at the end of the year.

And that's not all—Lapierre will be volunteering her time to teach textile design and sewing classes at the Center. "Volunteering my time for the Center's Christmas play was the most fun I've had in years. Costumes, like clothing, are important in helping young people feel confident, which positively impacts their entire life. Working with these young people inspires me. I think everyone will be shocked by the Liana Lapierre spring line—although luxurious fabrics and impeccable fit will continue, expect to see some urban influence as well," Lapierre explained.

We are looking forward to it! As always, expect the Post to keep you posted! (We will also have our eye on Lapierre's left ring finger...)

Ella closed the newspaper with a sigh. "That makes me so happy, I think I might burst." She turned and smiled at Wyatt.

"Sam and Liana, huh? I had a feeling when we saw them together at the party last night that things were pretty serious, didn't you?"

Ella nodded. "I did. And they're funding the community center? Bonnie must be over the moon. And Joana too!"

"I've always believed in Christmas miracles," Wyatt said, giving Ella a sideways glance. He caught her rolling her eyes.

The rest of the trip went by quickly and before they knew it, they were pulling up to a sprawling Victorian with a covered front porch spanning the entire length of the home. Ella grabbed Wyatt's hand and gave it a squeeze.

"I have one very important question before you go meet my family." Wyatt's face was serious, and Ella's eyebrows lifted in anticipation. "Did you remember to bring the pastelillos?"

Ella laughed and squeezed Wyatt's hand again. His words did the trick, she was relaxed and confident everything was going to work out like it was supposed to.

"I never dreamed I'd be back at home for Christmas again," Wyatt said softly. "And I certainly never dreamed I'd be here with someone as wonderful as you." He glanced up at his parents' house and then looked over at Ella.

"That's why you should never stop dreaming!"

THE END

ABOUT THE AUTHOR

Kate Kasch is the author of the Verity Townsend mystery series, which includes _Jane Street_ and _The Dakota,_ and two holiday romances, _Restoring Christmas_ and The Christmas Invitation.

She lives in northern New Jersey with her (amazing) husband and four non-stop children.

In order to stay sane, she writes and runs.

Learn more at www.katekasch.com

Made in the USA
Middletown, DE
19 November 2019

79035719R00128